The Greatest Comic Book Tale Ever Told

Michael Colon

2025, TWB Press

www.twbpress.com

The Greatest Comic Book Tale Ever Told
Copyright © 2025 by Michael Colon

Edited by Terry Wright

Cover Art by Terry Wright

ISBN: 978-1-967888-03-0

Prologue

I never get tired of this view overlooking the citizens of Irontown City. My office window is at the very top floor of the tallest skyscraper in the metropolitan area. From these heights, I can see the entire landscape of the city, and I find inspiration from these heights to continue my work. I'm grateful that I can make my city a better place. Superheroes in cartoons or comic books hover in the sky above their homes as guardian angels. I can't be everywhere at once, so I let my good work speak for me.

My job is to help people believe in their potential through the fantastical tales of good battling evil. Comic books make the world a better place, and my comic book production company is number one in the world. They give people hope in the fight against the forces of evil in their lives.

There is one special comic book issue I have just released. I'd kept it for myself all these years. I'm not sure why it has taken me so long to put this story into production. I suppose I didn't want it to be mass-copied and lose its sentimental value. Yeah. I know. That was selfish of me.

My desk phone rings.

The receptionist downstairs tells me that my special guest is here. I tell the receptionist to send her into my office. While I await her arrival, I open my precious comic book, a true story of the epic battle between good against evil. It starts when I was just a boy:

CHAPTER 1

I wake up to a gentle breeze on my face. Golden streams of light peek through my bedroom window blinds. The rays of sunshine remind me of the superhero from my dream. There was a fight between two beings. One represented good and the other evil. After the battle, the evil one took over. My home city was destroyed. At the end of the dream, a voice told me to wake up and that my story must go on with love and not hate, even though I'm not a hateful person. The sunbeams shine on my favorite superhero action figure tucked in bed next to me. I'm not sure if I'm still dreaming because my room looks like a colorful comic book panel.

I grab my action figure. "There are people that need to be saved." We jump out of bed, and I fly my hero toy around my room while imagining we have different worlds to visit. After defeating the evil villains behind my window curtains, in the closet, the dresser drawers, and under my bed, I land my action figure on top of my pillow. All superheroes need rest, and he deserves it for all the work he has done. Meanwhile, I lie on the floor with my comic book to escape into the fictional world of incredible beings who always find a way to save the day. Since I don't have any friends, I like to think these comic book heroes are my besties. If my life were a comic book that would be awesome.

Sara knocks on my bedroom door. "I'm leaving for work, sweetheart."

I toss my colorful book of crime fighters to the side, and run to open the door. I don't get to spend much time with Sara since she works two jobs to support us. I wish I could have more quality time with her. She's the only person besides Ruth and Walter who love me. My heart is warm to see her, but I sigh. "Are you coming home late again tonight?"

Sara kisses the top of my head. "Yes, sweetheart. I left some cash on the kitchen table. Stay out of trouble, okay?"

"You know I never get into any trouble. I'm not one of the bad guys."

"Yes. I know, my little angel. Love you."

From the front door, I watch Sara walk down the street to catch the only bus that comes in and out of District Seven.

The Greatest Comic Book Tale Ever Told

A homeless lady pushes her cart of belongings past the house. She looks at me with a scowl. "What are you looking at, little rat?"

For a moment, she turns into a monster, so I slam the front door shut and lock it. She's a reminder why I don't go outside to make friends. I'm better off staying inside, reading my comics or playing with my plastic hero. District Seven is also known as the landfill district. It is not a place to meet anybody friendly. District Seven is at the far edge of Irontown City, away from the other districts. I look at the neighborhood from my window. This place is in bad shape, including the people who roam in misery with no purpose. Sara is the only person who smiles in a district that looks like a war zone.

I open my comic book to gaze at the illustrations of defenders for justice fighting evil in a fantasy world. This is a world I'd rather exist in, but what superhero would want to be friends with a loser like me?

Pages flip, panels fly by, and I muster up the courage to walk outside. I'm a fourteen-year-old loser, headed to my favorite spot, the abandoned railroad yard. I keep my nose buried in my comic book. I'm afraid to give people eye contact because I know they don't like losers.

A man taps me on my shoulder. He has holes in his clothes and dirt on his face, looks like he hasn't eaten in days. With his shaking palms upturned toward me, he mumbles words I can't understand, but I know he wants me to drop some coins into his hands. I dig in my pockets and pull out a piece of gum and a few nickels and dimes. The money Sara left for me is at home, and it's only for an emergency. I drop the coins in his scarred hands, and his eyes light up as if I'd given him a bar of gold. He sits on the sidewalk and moves the coins around in his palms, mumbling to himself.

I keep walking, passing masked representatives who claim territory in District Seven. They are considered the evil villains around here. The people who wear these masks rarely show their faces because the person behind the mask is viewed as nothing to society.

At the abandoned railroad yard outside of the neighborhood, I climb inside an empty train cart to finish reading my comic book, alone. I do get sad sometimes that I don't have friends to share this spot with and read heroic stories. After reading my comic book, I sit in the middle of the shutdown railroad track with my legs crossed. Sara told me not to venture too far out past the tracks because that is where the landfill lies, and it's hazardous there. Some say monsters live in the mountains of trash. Most people of Irontown don't know what lies beyond the landfill. They'd rather let the garbage accumulate until all of us are buried in it.

I get up from the center of the train tracks and climb on top of one of the train carts with my action figure. I position my toy to sit beside me to watch the clouds float by. My action figure won't think I'm weird for sky gazing. If monsters or demons are real, then I know somewhere behind the clouds are heroes watching over us. Sara tells me there are angels who occasionally come down to help people.

I say to my action figure, "Thanks for hanging out with me." If I had the choice to have a super power for a day, it would be flight. I move my toy from side to side, repeating some cool lines from my comic books. After playing pretend, I jump down from the train cart, and as I leave the railroad yard, I see a man sitting on a blanket with wooden animal models. I hide behind another empty cart, hoping he won't see me.

"No need to be frightened of me," he says.

I peek around the cart. I don't know who I can

trust to be a good person around here. I should make a run for it. "I'm not allowed to talk to strangers."

"Your parents taught you well, but you are talking to me, right? You seem intrigued with my wooden models."

I walk closer to him, but remain a safe distance so I can run away if I have to.

"My name is Ralph," he says.

"My name is Sonny."

"We all need something we love to do to keep us going. If more people had something they love to do there wouldn't be as much violence here. We need more good people in this world." Ralph hands me his well-crafted wooden bird. Even the feathers and beak are flush in fine detail. "Do you believe superheroes like your toy exist?"

"I would like to believe they're real. Somebody has to be watching over us."

"If you happen to encounter a superhero, let him or her know about me because I can use some help. Thank you for being kind to me. People can be cruel in Irontown." Ralph coughs blood.

I back away a little while he finishes his coughing fit. "Do you need water?"

"Just let me know if you see any superheroes. I

would like my story to go on."

"Why don't you have a home to go to?"

Ralph wipes some blood off his chin and takes a deep breath. "Not everyone is fortunate to grow up with a family to love them and provide a home. I have been living out here for a long time."

"I'll come back with some food for you. I'll be right back."

I leave the railroad yard, still admiring the fine details carved into the wooden bird. I hope Ralph gets to have a home one day. Sleeping outside with nobody to cook him a meal is horrible. While walking home, I see something from the corner of my eye that I cannot explain. I look over and across the street and see these two transparent images fighting and fading into nothing. I cross the street and stand where I saw the two images going at it. I hear a thunderous boom in the sky and look up. I see a person wearing a cape fighting a creature high above me. I ask the homeless people sitting around the dumpsters if they see this, but they don't. The images fade away like before.

Back in my room, I put the wooden bird by my window, facing the sky. I look around at my comic posters taped to the walls. These posters have graphic art of some of the coolest moments from each comic book. Each moment shows a hero saving the day. Sara works extra hours to buy me comics that come with posters. I put my hand on a holographic poster that I cherish. I call the pizza shop and put in an order to have a pie delivered to the house with the money Sarah left. I lay on my bed and close my eyes, but as soon as I do I hear a menacing laugh in my room. I sit up in a black void. Shadow arms grab me from under the bed. I try to fight them off with my scrawny frame. I call for Sara to help me, but the shadow arms cover my mouth, and pull me under the bed where I see a terrifying face with red eyes and razor sharp teeth. Right before the face opens its mouth to eat me, I wake up in a sweat. I pull the covers over me and hold my hero action figure. Shaking with fear, I tell myself it was just a bad dream. I peek under the bed and don't see the monster.

I hear a knock on the door so I tiptoe and open it slightly to see the pizza man tapping his foot. I hand him the cash and was going to apologize for keeping him waiting, but he shoves the pizza box into my chest and leaves. After eating a couple slices of pizza, I wrap a few more for Ralph and walk back to the old railroad yard. There, I hear a commotion I'm not familiar with. I hide inside a train cart and see bad people who wear masks tormenting Ralph. They throw rocks at him and call him mean names. My stomach is in a knot from what I'm witnessing. I don't know what to do. Do I stand here and watch Ralph get bullied? I should ignore this and walk back home. As I back away, I step on a plastic bottle that makes a crunch noise. The bad people messing with Ralph turn their attention to me.

Ralph shouts, "Sonny, run!"

My legs are locked in place so I can't run even though I want to. The bad people walk toward me. For a moment they turn into monsters and back to people. They surround me, leaving me with an inch of space to move. Shaking in fear, I drop the wrapped up pizzas on the ground.

One of them asks, "You got a problem with what we did to the old geezer?"

"I just want to go home."

They laugh at what I said like the pathetic weakling I am. They throw me to the ground and pummel me with punches and kicks while I curl up in a ball. The reason why I'm in this situation is because I can't defend myself. I'm not strong, and the weak get taken advantage of. They stop hitting me, and one of the bad people takes my comic book and rips it to shreds. As they leave, I get some parting kicks to my body, and they take the wrapped pizzas. I remain in a fetal position, whimpering. I look up at the sky while my body is throbbing in pain, waiting for an angel that Sara says will come down to comfort me.

"Don't cry, Sonny," Ralph says. "You have a home to go back to. I have to suffer this type of abuse from the world every day."

"I'm sorry that this happened, Ralph." I pick up the shreds of my comic book and let them fall out of my hands.

"So pathetic," someone says. Standing in front of me is a shadow with red eyes and a smile full of razor sharp teeth.

"If only you would wake up and let me in. I can make you strong beyond your imagination. You would no longer worry about how to defend yourself."

"Who are you?"

The ominous shadow in the shape of a person puts its hands on my shoulders.

I shiver from the ice cold touch spreading throughout me. The shadow disappears, and I limp away to more strife repeating on every street I pass. The same illustrations of starving people on the

The Greatest Comic Book Tale Ever Told

sidewalk and going through trash cans. I start to cry because of what happened to me and Ralph. I look at the blurry sky behind my tear filled eyes, hoping a hero will come down to give me words of encouragement. A few raindrops fall from the sky. I stop walking and let the water hit me. Is God crying for me from heaven? I stand in front of my broken home with black clouds above me. The black clouds make it seem like I'm cursed. Flashes of lightning surge above, but they don't look like ordinary lightning. These electrical surges of energy seem to come from these people fighting in the sky. Between breaks in dark clouds, I see people fighting monsters in the sky, shooting out the energy surges. A bolt of lightning strikes down on the street near me. I run inside.

In my room, I bury my face in my pillow to cry more than the rain outside because of how weak I am. I must have cried myself to sleep, because when I lift my head from my tear-soaked pillow I'm at a cemetery with bumpy cobblestone pathways going in different directions. This cemetery has hundreds of walkways and thousands of indigo flower petals blowing around. I have no idea how I got here, so I call out to Sara for help, but get no response. A bright yellow flower petal floats by, and I follow it. The golden flower petal lands at my feet, but as I pick it up, it blows away again. I follow the yellow petal to a couple graves. The millions of indigo flower petals lift off the ground and disintegrate to ashes. There is a rose in my hand that I don't remember having with me, and I can't read the names on the headstones. I kneel down to try to read the blurry names, and Sara taps me on the shoulder.

"You need to wake up. You must have had a bad dream." She turns to ashes, and the cemetery turns to dust, leaving me in a black void.

The shadow comes over while I'm helplessly on my knees. "Aren't you tired of being insignificant yet?" The shadow holds the sides of my head. Its hands are so cold.

I place my hands on its hands and look into its bright red eyes. I try to pull its hands off my head but they won't budge. I jerk my body in every way to break free of its grip and scream for help. I wake up screaming on the bedroom floor with Sara trying to calm me down.

"Sonny, my sweet baby boy, it's okay. I'm here. You must have had a bad dream."

I jump out of her arms and sit back on the bed,

The Greatest Comic Book Tale Ever Told

staring at my hero action figure. Sara sits next to me, wearing her work clothes. She must have just gotten home.

"You had a horrible dream. Do you want to talk about it?"

"I rather not, Sara. I'm ready for bed."

Sara gets up. "You can talk to me about anything. That's why I'm here." She closes the door.

I grab my action figure to keep me company in the shower. I can't stay in the shower long because I'll use up the only hot water we are allowed to have daily. The cool thing about this action figure is that I don't recognize it from any comic books I read. This action figure is its own character design without being copied from somewhere else. The golden design and red cape is so cool. It feels like I know this hero from somewhere. Has to be from another comic story.

I step out of the shower and see something that doesn't make sense. A tear in reality. I've only seen this from cartoons. Leading out of the bathroom is a comic-style drawn frame. This tear in reality shows a world being drawn in real-time with me on the bus heading to Walter and Ruth's. I hold both sides of the comic panel and think to myself that I have to be dreaming still. I stick my head through the panel, and a world sketches itself, getting colored in. I hold my breath and jump through the frame.

I'm now dressed and on the bus on my way to Walter and Ruth's. They are Sara's parents. They treat me like I'm their biological grandson. I stare out the bus window, watching the same sad story repeat on every street corner. I open my comic book to escape my surroundings. If I can fly I wouldn't have to take the bus across the garbage district. I yearn to know what a hero feels when soaring around the clouds.

I get off the bus and knock on their door.

Ruth opens the door with the same smile Sara has. "Our favorite grandson is here to pay us a visit. Come inside, sweetie. I'll make your favorite tea."

I step inside their small cozy living space that has antiques from their childhood. I walk over to my favorite antique while Ruth calls for Walter. This antique is a bronze birdcage with a wooden baby blue jay glued to its perch. I bet Ralph can make that.

I sit on their purple leather couch, looking up at the hanging pictures of them when they were younger. With shaking hands, Ruth serves me her homemade herbal tea. I help Ruth by taking the tea cups and silverware from her so she won't spill it.

She sits down next to me, holding her lower back

and grimacing. "Don't be in a rush to get old, Sonny."

"I will get old one day."

"Yes you will. So enjoy your youth while you have it. Youth is often wasted on the young."

Walter comes in, wearing his tool belt and back-brace. "Hello, grandson. When you're done with your tea you can help me with a project."

I always enjoy helping Walter with his projects. While we work together, he tells the coolest stories from back in his time. I finish my tea and go out to their small backyard. On the fence, a family of birds watches Walter hand me some nails and wood. He shows me where to place the boards and how to hammer nails properly. While helping him with the birdhouse, he tells me how doing things the right way is important. It's hard and honest work. According to him, Irontown City is a place where many want to be famous or wealthy overnight, but they've forgotten the ways of being humble and building their lives from the ground up. The family of birds watches us build their new home. When we finish, the birds fly happily into the birdhouse.

Walter and I walk to a vacant baseball field that has garbage all over it to play catch. Most parks in district seven are not taken care of and not safe from the broken glass and toxic materials. At one point playing catch with Walter, I let the baseball land beside me while looking up at the sky.

"Grandson, what are you looking at?"

"I was imagining what it would feel like to fly like the heroes in my comics."

"You sure do love those comic books. I guess reading as many as you do will make you wonder about that. If I read as many comic books as you, I'd probably start seeing things too." What Sara, Ruth, and Walter don't know is that I feel without a purpose in this world. I never expressed this to anyone, and it's becoming more difficult to hold in. After playing catch, we walk back to their place and they share more stories about the good old days. It seems like those days were a better time to live in Irontown. It's getting late, and Sara doesn't like me traveling back at night, and neither do I. I say my goodbyes to Walter and Ruth and take the cross-district bus home.

As the sun sets, I stand outside of my home. I look both ways in the middle of the street, close my eyes, and tilt my head back, trying to find the feeling of being weightless. I raise my arms, and my body feels light. I think about elevating off the street. For a moment, I feel myself floating up. I open my eyes and my feet remain flat on the street. I lower my arms and go inside.

Early the following morning, Sara puts my church outfit together. While she adjusts my collar, I feel like my life is not my own. It's like the days go by while my world mimics a comic book, and the pages turn for me, and I unwillingly have to go along with it. Sara always says that we need to honor God for providing us with what we have. I look at myself in the mirror and feel uncomfortable in my church outfit. I'm never confident with how I look. She says we have to look presentable for church as respect toward God's house.

On the cross-district bus going to the only church in District Seven, Sara prays quietly. It sounds like she is mumbling to herself. If God is real and watching over us with the angels, then superheroes have to be real, too. Perhaps they're hiding, and only come out when we get lucky enough to get a quick glimpse of them. People who live in District Seven of Irontown are looked at as second-class citizens, so we aren't worth being saved by the angels or heroes.

When Sara finishes praying I ask, "Is God the strongest hero of them all?"

"God is more than a superhero. He is everything

that makes up love and life."

We get off the bus and stand in front of St. Michael's Church, which has big black iron doors with carvings of angels celebrating.

"Why are the angels celebrating?"

"They celebrate because of the love and mercy God has for creation. When we have faith that God will provide for us, life becomes so much better. The same way you have faith in the idea of superheroes saving the day from evildoers, we need to have more faith in what God will bless us with."

"So if I ask God to make me strong, will I be able to protect us?"

Sara takes my hand as we walk toward the tall iron doors. "You're already strong."

At the main hall of the cathedral there is a long red carpet going down the aisle with lots of chairs on each side. We walk past people bowing their heads and praying while holding onto each other. We sit near the front of the altar, and Sara prays some more. I should try. I fold my hands and close my eyes.

"Dear God, I want to be strong just like a superhero from my comics. I want to be able to fly because that's my favorite superpower. I want to meet a real-life hero who can give me some of their powers so I won't be so pathetic." I open my eyes and close them again. "Oh yeah. Amen."

I don't hear God answer back. Sara goes over to console other members of the church while I sit, looking at the altar. A stranger taps me on the shoulder and welcomes me to the church. Sara says I shouldn't be rude by just staring and not saying anything back when someone greets me.

"Nice to meet you too," I mumble.

I walk over to the stained glass window of angels flying around a bright golden light. Sara comes over to marvel at the stained glass window with me. I want to tell her how worthless I feel, but I don't want to make her sad. I'll keep these feelings to myself. Bottled up inside me. We sit down.

The preacher walks to the altar. He takes the microphone, and everyone's eyes are locked on this man. For the next hour, the preacher talks about the real world and the spiritual world. How good and evil cross the boundaries of our world in an everlasting war that involves us, God's creations. The preacher goes on to mention how our stories don't end here if we do the right things in God's eyes. This preaching sounds similar to the tales from my comic books. The Devil is supposed to be the most powerful evil villain and wants people to go against God who is the leader of love and justice. After the message, Sara asks the priest for an additional prayer so we can make it home safely. We all hold hands, and before I close my eyes, I see the shadow figure with red eyes in the far corner of the church. I keep one eye open on the ominous shadow being. It's smiling at me. After they both say amen, I do as well, and the shadow disappears.

We leave the church, and as I ask Sara questions about the angels, I see these people suspended high in the sky. I rip my hand away from Sara's, and run to where they are in the sky, hoping for a better look. While running, I trip over a lip in the sidewalk and hurt my elbow. Sara runs over to me and goes through her purse to tend to my wound. She takes my elbow and pats it with alcohol pads, wipes the blood with tissues, and places a bandage on my sore elbow.

"Sweetie, what on earth were you running to?"

I look back up at the empty sky, and those people are gone. "I thought I saw the angels you talk about."

At home, we share a meal that we try to make tradition since she is always working. After eating, Sara leaves for her night part-time job. In bed, I stare at the ceiling until my eyes get heavy. I get out of my bed in a hallway that has ice all over it. Every breath I take I can see in front of me. In my visible breath these words tell me to wake up and come home.

I open my eyes to the sun coming up. Beneath my feet is another comic panel to fall into, of me and Sara on the bus to District One of Irontown City. Is my life really my own? Do I have a purpose? Is someone turning the pages, and I have to follow like a puppet? Because I'm so weak? What does it matter? I fall through the panel, and I'm suddenly with Sara, heading to District One. District One is also known as the Metro District, which is the heart of Irontown City. The Metro District of Irontown is one of the most modern and technology rich metropolises in the world. It's full of big businesses. District One is always jammed packed with traffic, and constant digital advertising flashes on the skyscrapers. We get off the bus to millions of Irontown's citizens marching in all directions. Nobody in this city gives each other eye contact unless it's of convenience to the individual. We get to where the city's piers are, where I'll see my first fireworks show. Cargo ships float by with steam emitting from them. I lean over the railing on the pier and imagine myself flying away to see where these cargo boats go. The sun sets, and now there are thousands looking up for the first fireworks to explode above us.

"Sara. Do you ever feel like you're supposed to be doing something more in this life?"

"I felt that way before. But when I picked you up from the orphanage, that feeling went away."

"I've been having these weird dreams."

"What kind of dreams?"

"It's hard to describe. It's like my dreams are trying to tell me something."

"Dreams are like a window into our soul. Our consciousness. Dreams are an alternate reality we create. They're another gift from God we are blessed with."

"Like a superpower?"

"Yes. Like a superpower, my little superhero boy."

The first fireworks whiz into the air. One by one, rockets explode, lighting up the night sky. I can feel the vibration from the explosions in my chest. As everyone cheers, I think about what Sara said about dreams. These fireworks are so amazing that I can't take my eyes off them. I hope I get to have dreams about fireworks. Every time they go off, for a brief moment, I see these beings floating in the shade of the night sky, then they disappear. I lean closer over the railing, trying to understand what I see in the fireworks' bright colorful patterns. If those are heroes, I wonder if they're enjoying this show as much as I am. My world folds over multiple times, like pages turning in a comic book, until summer ends.

The pages stop flipping, and I sit on the foot of my bed, twiddling my thumbs. I feel like I just go through the motions. Summer went by so fast. Like time fast-forwarded without me wanting it to. My nerves are flaring since today is the first day I go to public school with normal kids. This is the start of a new chapter. Although I'm starting my education with other students in a public school system, I know for a fact I won't be able to make any friends.

Sara comes into my room before going to work and sits beside me, knowing I'm nervous. She says a mother has this thing called intuition and can sense how I'm feeling. I guess she has a superpower. Even though Sara isn't my biological mother, I know she loves me more than anything in this world.

"Sonny, before I go to work I want to tell you that you will do great in school. You will make friends. Just be yourself." She runs her hands through my messy hair. "No matter how much I comb your hair, it finds a way to be messy."

Before she leaves, I latch onto her for a hug. "I know I have to get my education, but I do wish I can read my comics all day. I'll try to be brave for you."

"The superheroes you admire will be proud of you for starting this new chapter, the same way I am." Sara gives me a kiss and leaves to work.

I pack notebooks and pencils in my superhero bookbag she bought for me. This bookbag has my favorite crime fighters on it. I stuff my toy into my bag, as well. Before going to where the school bus will pick me up, I go to the abandoned railroad yard to see if Ralph came back. The spot where Ralph would sit with his wooden animal models is still vacant. I guess I'll never see him again. I want to tell him that I'm starting a new chapter in my life.

I walk back to my neighborhood to wait for the bus and see ripples in the bright blue cartoon-looking sky. I hold the straps of my bookbag tight to my body as the school bus approaches.

The driver stops. "Hey, kid. I hate coming around this district. Hurry and get on."

I step into the school bus and look at the floor while walking down the aisle to the back corner seat. I open my bookbag and stare at my golden hero toy

The Greatest Comic Book Tale Ever Told

while taking deep breaths. I press the button on its chest to make it light up like the sun. I feel a little better, but the school bus hits a bump on the road, and my toy goes flying out of my hand and lands in the aisle.

One student yells, "Aww. You like to play with dolls."

Everyone laughs at me while I quickly scrambled to get my action figure. I keep my face in my bookbag, trying not to cry for the rest of the ride.

The bus driver shouts, "Do you mind getting off the bus? I want to grab some breakfast."

I hurry off the bus and look back at the annoyed driver. He rolls his eyes at me and speeds off, leaving me in a cloud of dust. Clutching the straps of my bag, I look at the place where I'll start the new chapter of my life, Irontown High School.

There's a giant rip in the sky, like it's made of paper. I've never seen anything like that before. It looks like a glitch in a video game.

There are many students outside the campus grounds, wearing different hair styles. I can't move my legs to walk to the doors because of fear. A group of students bump into me, snapping me out of it.

I enter Irontown High and to my first class of the

day. I sit in the back corner near the window and watch my classmates fill the desks. The teacher comes into the classroom and announces everyone's name. I look out the window, and that rip in the world folds over my way like a giant paper wave.

The teacher asks, "Sonny Forever, are you here?"

I raise my hand. "I'm here."

I hear the loud sound of a page turn.

CHAPTER 2

I always prefer to get to my classes early, before my classmates arrive. I use that time to study and read my comic books since I'm not allowed to escape into the world of good versus evil when class begins. I look out the classroom window at the sky, thinking about the feeling of flight and how cool it would be. I look back at the desk, and my comic book is gone. These hateful words that I tend to think toward myself carve themselves into the desk. On the chalkboard in front of the classroom the phrase, wake up, writes itself multiple times in chalk. I jump up from my desk and run to the front door to get out, but I can't open it. I pull the doorknob, yelling for help. The shadow person steps out of the blackboard, holding the comic book I was just reading. The ominous being tears the comic in half and demands I wake up.

I wake up with the side of my face planted on the desk. I quickly look up at the chalkboard, and Ms. Weizmann enters the classroom with her hair a mess, holding a giant stack of papers. She slams her papers down on her desk and takes a long sip of coffee from her canister that has happy-face stickers on it.

She looks at me then looks at the chalkboard. "Is something wrong with the blackboard, Sonny?"

"Nothing is wrong. I must have dozed off. I had a weird dream."

She nods. "You know what they say about dreams. They're a window into another world."

As my classmates fill the room, I keep my head down, doodling a stick figure hero saving the day. None of my classmates talk to me because they think I'm weird. Sara says I should try to be social, but I can't get myself to do that. Every time I see a classmate and think of saying hello, fear of rejection pulls me back.

During class we are called to the front for participation points, which I hate doing. I do hope the bell rings before I get called up to the front. Ms. Weizmann calls me to come up even though I'm hunched over behind my classmate. Beads of sweat develop on my forehead as I get up and walk to the board. I grab a piece of chalk and drop it on the floor because my hands are clammy. I bend over to pick it up, and someone makes a fart noise. Everyone starts laughing.

Ms. Weizmann shouts at the class to quiet down.

I wipe sweat off my forehead and proceed to solve the equation. Every time the chalk hits the board, I hear my classmates laughing in my mind. Their laughs become distorted, turning into monster cackles. I place the chalk down and face the class with my head down.

"Sonny, please explain to the class how you solved the problem?"

I tilt my head up, and my classmates' faces are hard to look at. They look like they want me to drop dead where I stand.

I barely look at Ms. Weizmann. "I'm sorry I can't do that." I go back to my desk and watch everyone go up to the board and explain how they solved their math problem. Why can't I be as good as these students?

The bell rings, and everyone sprints to the door. I wait for them to leave before slowly packing my books into my bag.

Before I leave the classroom, Ms. Weizmann tells me that she wants to have a word with me. I sit down looking at my hands folded while she sits at a desk next to me.

"You're not in trouble, but as your teacher, I have to ask why you always avoid participation. You're doing great on your tests, and you understand the lesson material. But you avoid participating at all costs. Let's try to be better at being involved in the classroom. One day at a time."

"Thank you, Ms. Weizmann. I'll try harder." I leave her classroom and walk down the hall. Ahead, I see a group of bullies who usually pick on me. They wear black leather jackets, and chains hang from their jeans. When we cross paths, they push me out of their way because they know I won't do anything, and they're right. I'm not strong enough to stick up for myself. I continue toward the school's exit, holding the straps of my bookbag tight to my body, anxious from everyone looking at me.

Off the campus grounds, all the students gather into their groups. I'm too different to be part of any group, so I don't bother to approach them. I tap my forehead, realizing I left one of my comic books in my locker.

I run back into the school and open my locker as fast as I can. I don't want to miss the first school bus. As soon as I open the door, the bullies grab me and slam me against the row of lockers. While the bullies hold my fragile body against the wall, Tommy, their leader, walks over to me. "Sonny, shouldn't you be going home on the school bus?" Tommy and his gang of bullies had it out for me since I started freshman year. Behind Tommy and his friends, I see the shadow person watching me with its arms crossed, shaking its head.

"What are you looking at over there, weirdo?"

"Please let me go. I know after hours this hall is your turf. I swear I was going to leave." Tommy and his bully friends toss me into an empty locker and lock it shut. I watch them laughing through the slits, leaving me here alone.

The shadow person approaches the slits of the locker. Inside this enclosed space with my chest tightening, all I think about is how I'll never get out of here. I pound on the locker, but because I'm so weak, I won't be able to break out.

The shadow says, "I want you to look at me and push on the door."

I look into its red glowing eyes, and rage fills me. I shove the locker door from the inside, causing it to fly off and hit the wall across from me. The shadow is gone.

A school dean walks by. "Are you okay?"

Michael Colon

I don't have time to process how I did that. I need to catch the school bus. I ignore the dean and run outside, frantically waving my arms to get the bus driver's attention. The bus doors swing open and the driver looks at me with an angry glare. I sit in the back of the bus and look out the window as students get off at their stops. I wish I could fight back against those bullies, but how was I able to do that to the locker? By the time we reach the landfill district I'm alone on the bus.

While walking home, I notice an elderly woman struggling with her belongings. She's wearing worn out dirty clothes like most people here.

"Ma'am, do you need any help with those bags?"

"That will be very nice of you, young man. Most people around here don't do nice things for others." This lady reminds me of Ruth. I can never take advantage and hurt someone else, even though it's done to me. I help her home with her stuff and she thanks me a few more times. It feels nice to do good for others. Heroes must feel this all the time.

In my bedroom, I put my bookbag on the floor and start my homework. My papers fall off the bed from a sudden shaking. Is there an earthquake going on? I run to my window and see a two-story-high monster stomping by. A few heroes, fading in and out, swarm the giant. This can't be real. As I open my window, the giant and heroes erase away.

When I finish my assignments and studying, another comic book panel draws itself in front of me. I guess I have no choice but to go through. I step into the frame, and I'm sitting on the back of the school bus with other students occasionally looking back at me, making remarks about my bookbag, or the clothes I wear. I open my comic book, and the first page is black with a pair of red eyes looking at me. I turn the pages and they repeat with the same eyes. I frantically turn the pages, hearing some students make more comments about me. I look up to see faces of disgust turn toward me. I look down at my comic book, and it's back to normal.

"What are you reading?" this girl asks across from me.

"It's just a picture book." It's hard for me to trust others, and I expect her to be in on some cruel joke. She hasn't made a mean comment yet.

"That is a cool picture book. Are you okay with me sitting next to you? My name is Marylee. I just transferred here a few days ago."

"My name is Sonny. Yes you can."

Marylee has thick glasses and braces on her teeth. I wonder if she feels like an outcast like me, considering she told me she is new. I keep my head turned out the window, avoiding eye contact with her. I'm not use to another student being this nice to me.

Marylee says, "I understand that you're extremely shy, and you don't trust a lot of people. I hear how the other students talk about you. I don't think you're any of those bad things. I would like to read your cool picture book someday. I have never seen one like that before."

We get off the bus and I hurry to be alone.

***

Before the school day officially begins, I sit in the cafeteria at a table in the back, looking at everyone socializing. I know better than to join in at any of the lunch tables because I'm too different. Students gossip about how I look and what I'm wearing. They don't care that I can hear them, so I leave the cafeteria. Walking down the school hallway alone, I kick a crumpled paper ball in front of me, but it accidentally bounces off someone's shoe. I look up and see Tommy with his bully friends. Next thing I know, I'm getting dragged into the boys' bathroom.

The Greatest Comic Book Tale Ever Told

Tommy says to his gang of bullies, "We need to teach Sonny a lesson. How dare he kick that garbage at us. Only people from his district should have garbage thrown at them. They are garbage."

"It was just an accident."

Tommy punches me in the stomach.

I fall to my knees, holding my gut. While catching my breath, the bullies pick me up and force me into the bathroom stall. Tommy pushes my head down toward the water, and I hold the side of the seat so my face won't go into the toilet, but it's getting hard to hold on.

Tommy leans in to my ear. "Say sorry."

"I'm sorry."

Being the flimsy person I am, he easily tosses me out of the stall and growls, "After school. The back parking lot. If you don't show, I'll shove your face all the way into the dirty toilet water next time." Tommy leaves with his bully friends.

I quickly exit the bathroom, feeling ashamed and violated. I can't look anyone in their eyes. While looking down, I bump into Marylee.

"Hey, Sonny, are you okay?"

I wipe the tears forming in my eyes and hurry out. Before I can make a run for the school bus, Tommy and the bullies drag me to the back of the building. I was foolish for thinking I could get away from them. Tommy forces me to duck behind a teacher's car. With a menacing grin, he takes out something wrapped in tissue paper.

"You see that fat boy over there? We call him Fat Franklin, and we have a special gift for him." Tommy unwraps the tissue paper carefully from around a stink bomb that emits a foul odor. He hands it to me. "You're going to throw this at Fat Franklin, and if you don't, I hope you have a thirst for toilet water."

The trauma of this moment is causing the colors of my world to melt away. Like a painting over a furnace, the colors warp and leak downward. With the stink bomb in my hands, I shake with fear, knowing if I mess this up they will hurt me. If I had known public school would be like this, I would have never come.

I throw the stink bomb, but miss on purpose so it won't hit this poor student who has no idea what's going on. Even with the bullies threatening me, I still can't hurt another person.

Tommy and his friends slap me on the head and run away.

I run from the school parking lot, and Franklin

The Greatest Comic Book Tale Ever Told follows me. My world isn't warped and melting around me anymore. Franklin and I stop, hold our knees, out of breath, a safe distance away.

Franklin takes an asthma inhaler and uses it so he can breathe. "Are you part of Tommy's crew? I don't have any more lunch money to give."

"I'm not a bully. In fact, they bully me too."

"They call me Fat Franklin, Frankfurter Franklin, or Flubber Frank. Those names are hurtful, but I brush them off."

"I would never call you those names. That is so mean."

"Well maybe we can be buddies? I only have one other friend here at Irontown High." Franklin holds out his fist, and I give him a fist-bump. "Now it's official. Nothing is stronger than the fist-bump of friendship."

Marylee comes over to us and looks surprised to see me. She gives Franklin a hug. "You two know each other?"

He uses his asthma inhaler again.

"Franklin, why are you having a near asthma attack?" She is very concerned for him.

"We had to run away from Tommy and the bullies."

"You two have to be careful. We still have three years before graduation."

Franklin coughs. "How about we all be friends?"

Marylee is all smiles. "I think that's a great idea."

Just like Sara said, I made my first friends at school. We walk to the pick up spot for the school buses, and I get on the last one. Sara always gives me some emergency money just in case I have to take public transit back to District Seven.

When I get off the bus, I step into a panel that turns day to later that night. Sara, still in her work clothes, is sleeping on the couch. She must have passed out as soon as she got in.

I lean in and whisper, "Am I an accident? Do I have a purpose in this world? I have so many questions about why I'm here. Will you forget about me the way my parents did? Why didn't you leave me at the orphanage?" I give her a kiss on the forehead.

When I go into my bedroom, I step into tomorrow's panel at the school cafeteria. Marylee sits at my table and we give each other the fist-bump of friendship. "Can I see your cool picture book now?"

I move my arms from the comic book and slide it over to her. She holds it close to her face as if intrigued by what she is reading.

Franklin comes up from behind and startles her by shouting good morning in her ear.

She jumps. "Franklin, you jerk," then punches him in the arm a couple times.

Marylee hits hard. I wouldn't want to make her angry.

She waves the comic book. "Are there any girl heroes in these stories?"

"Of course there are."

Franklin says to me, "I wonder what their superpowers are? Maybe it's being annoying."

Marylee hits Franklin's arm again.

Some of Marylee's girlfriends come over to our table. She clears her throat loud enough for us to hear. "Franklin, are you going to walk me to class and carry my books?"

Marylee's friends giggle amongst each other while Marylee waits, tapping her shoe.

Franklin gets up to help Marylee with her books. "She thinks she is my boss. I'll catch up with you soon, Sonny."

As I walk down the halls, I hear Marylee yell out, "Franklin, you're disgusting."

A few seconds later, Franklin runs to me.

"What happened?"

"I was gassy and I couldn't hold it in. You would think the way she treats me she like-likes me."

"Maybe she does like-like you."

Franklin notices my comic book. "Hey, Sonny. You think I can borrow one of those comic books? They are really cool."

I open my bookbag and give Franklin an extra one. His eyes light up as he flips through the pages. "Imagine what kind of world we would live in if these heroes and villains were real."

I tear a page from my comic and fold it as small as I can, then place it in Franklin's hands. "Hide this in a place that will be difficult for anyone to find. Whoever finds it will be a superhero who reveals himself to us."

"I'll put this somewhere no one will ever find."

I give Franklin a fist-bump, and after school, all three of us take the bus downtown to District One. This is our first hangout date as friends. We stand in front of the giant glass display of upcoming comic book releases. So many beautiful glossy covers of fascinating stories ready to be told. Stories of people doing the impossible. The best stories ever told.

We hear cop cars drive by us, sirens blaring. When they stop, the cops get out and chase a man

The Greatest Comic Book Tale Ever Told

holding a pile of jewelry. Rings and necklaces fall onto the street. In the skyscrapers' glass reflection I see these humanoids fly in the direction the robber is running.

We enter the comic shop and bells chime.

Oswald, the owner, stops sweeping the floor. "Welcome, kids. Anything I can help you with?"

"Hey, Oswald, no thanks. We are just browsing for now."

Marylee finds a comic book about a female hero. Franklin finds one about a hero who is muscular and can run really fast at supersonic speeds. I walk over to this small section of the shop dedicated to telling stories about evil villains. Why should villains have their own section amongst the good guys?

"You like what you see?" a deep menacing voice says in my ear. I turn around, but nobody is behind me. That voice sounds familiar.

I go back to my friends, and they're reading the sample comic books they picked out. It makes me happy to see them interested in what I love. "Do you guys live with your parents?"

Franklin answers, "I live with my aunt and uncle. My mom and dad travel for work. They own a shipping company, so they're always away."

Marylee says, "I live with my mother, father, and cousins. My mom and dad are first generation immigrants from the east. My cousins and I moved to Irontown as kids because of the unfair politics of where my parents are from."

I decide to be honest with them. "I never told you guys this because I wasn't sure if you'd accept me. Especially being from District Seven. I don't know anyone related to me. Sara is my foster mother. Also, this is my first time attending public school with students my age. I was afraid to tell both of you because I didn't want to lose the only friends I probably will make." They're both quiet and didn't react to what I said. I grab a superhero toy from off the shelf. "These heroes are people who don't look down on me."

Marylee takes the action figure out of my hands and puts it back. "The fact that you admitted all of that to us shows bravery. Like a superhero."

Franklin says, "I'm glad that we are still friends."

We leave the comic shop, and Franklin walks Marylee back home since they both live downtown in the Metro District. I catch the bus to my outcast district. I miss my friends already. When I get off the bus, another panel draws itself in front of me. I step

The Greatest Comic Book Tale Ever Told

over the border and into the panel that takes me to a school trip during my freshman year. Before the panel closes, for a second, I see a group of people wearing black suits, watching me until it closes.

As the school buses line up to bring us to the Irontown Planetarium, the classes of students get into single file lines. Some of my classmates point and laugh at me for the bookbag I have on. I don't wear the cool and up-to-date brands of clothes most others wear. I put my head down, and as I walk onto the bus, Marylee and Franklin sneak into my line so we can all sit near each other. I feel like we were just at the comic shop yesterday.

Franklin sits next to me.

Marylee rolls her eyes. "Oh, so you're going to leave poor little old me alone?"

I tell Franklin, "Go sit next to your girlfriend."

Marylee gasps. "No way, Sonny. Franklin is not my boyfriend."

"I'm not that bad looking. Sheesh." He sits next to her anyway.

The teacher announces, "Settle down, kids. We're off to the planetarium."

Everyone cheers while I lightly clap my hands.

During the ride, Franklin ignores Marylee as she

tries to talk to him. He's playing his handheld video game, so she sits next to me. "What are you thinking about? You've been staring at the sky for a while without looking at anything around you."

"I'm just daydreaming about the heroes from my comics doing circles around the clouds. I've been seeing characters from my comics in real life. Maybe it's my imagination."

"You have a big imagination."

"I guess I do. Have you ever wondered what your place is in this world?"

"I never really thought of that, to be honest. Did something happen at school before the trip? You better not lie to me."

"Nothing happened. It's just something I think about."

"We are going on our first school trip together. Think about all the cool stuff we will see instead of why you were born. Okay?"

"Sure, Marylee."

She falls asleep on my shoulder, and Franklin falls asleep with his video game in hand. I watch the green pastures go by in District Two, which is the farming and agriculture district. I hear these voices mumble from outside the window. I open the bus

The Greatest Comic Book Tale Ever Told

window, and I hear conversations about not wanting this story to end. Are those voices in the sky the angels that Sara says are real?

My eyes are heavy while looking at the rays of light piercing through the clouds like glowing swords. I wonder if that light comes from heaven. Heaven must be a beautiful place.

The rocking motion of the bus makes me sleepy. I close my eyes, then open them, and everyone is gone. At the front of the bus stands the shadow person I keep seeing. Nobody is driving, but the steering wheel is turning left and right. I walk down the aisle. On the fogged up windows, words tell me to wake up. It gets colder as I get closer to the phantom with bright red eyes.

"Who are you?" I ask.

The moment I touch the ominous figure, the temperature around me gets so cold I can see my breath. The bus hits a bump in the road, and I wake up to Franklin throwing a paper ball at Marylee.

"You're something else," Marylee says.

The bus stops, and a teacher stands up to announce we've arrived. Everyone cheers, and I sit in a daze, thinking about the dream I just had.

Marylee nudges me. "Remember. Let's enjoy our

trip." We all get off the school bus.

I'm stunned with how the planetarium looks. I've never seen a building shaped like this before. It kinda looks like a space station.

We walk into the planetarium theater where I sit between my two friends, holding their hands. The theater darkens as our seats recline back. An artificially created universe sparkles above us. The simulation starts, and we go on a 3D ride through the solar system as a voice guides us on our space journey. After the virtual space journey through black holes and around planets, we are free to roam the rest of the planetarium. My friends and I go to the discount shop. Sara had given me a few bucks to spend so I wouldn't feel left out. I notice something sparkle out of the corner of my eye on the discount rack. These crescent moon necklaces are cool. On the back of the half moon pendant are thoughtful words engraved: With love from the moon and back. We buy matching moon necklaces and tap them together. This is our official necklace of friendship, as corny as that may sound.

Back on the school bus, as the other students talk about what they experienced at the planetarium, I play with the moon pendant. I look at Marylee and

Franklin sitting next to each other, sleeping peacefully. I wonder what they are dreaming about. Do they have the same dreams I have?

The school bus drops me off, and the stars are out tonight, which is rare because of all the pollution here. I sit on the steps outside my home, holding my moon pendant, and see lights streak across the sky and do maneuvers. The shooting stars I learned about on the trip don't do that. The starlight gets lower. It looks like the entire sky of stars is floating above me. I reach up, and the stars take on a human shape. Before I know what they are, multiple pages turn around and through me. Like the world is blinking rapidly.

Now I sit at the dinner table in our dining room with a Happy Birthday card in front of me. I feel a loving warmth as I open the card from Sara. Some money falls out. I read the card:

"My son, I can't believe you're fourteen years old today. I made a promise when I first held your hand at the orphanage that I would always be there for you. I'm glad you love me like you love the superheroes in your comic books. I'm so proud of how good you're doing in school, and I'll never stop believing in you. Happy Birthday, sweetheart."

I sit in front of our house, looking at the broken

people in this broken world with trash all over. They drag themselves aimlessly to more pain and suffering. I wonder if they would be happier if they had someone make them a nice birthday card.

Sara walks up to me with a bag of groceries, and I give her a big hug.

"Happy Birthday, sweetie. I got some stuff to bake you a cake later. Ruth and Walter are coming over too. I made a promise to take you to see your parents. So let's go before they come over."

We take a few buses out of District Seven to where my parents have been for quite some time. Sara told me a while ago that my biological parents passed away, and although she showed me the official documents, this is my first time going to the cemetery. After a few bus rides, we reach Indigo Cemetery. We walk along the cobblestone paths that have millions of indigo colored flower petals blowing around. This place is just like I dreamed it would be. Actually, this cemetery looks very dream-like. I remember Ruth telling me that dreams are a window into the reality we can only visit when we go to sleep. A bright yellow flower petal floats over to us. This cemetery is bright and has a slight blurriness to it.

Sara says, "I have never seen any other colored

flower petals around here. That one must be the only one like it."

I snag the yellow petal out of the air, then let it go. Near us is a family celebrating around one of the graves.

I ask Sara, "Shouldn't they be sad?"

"There is a time to mourn and a time to celebrate life. Perhaps that family is reflecting on the good times with their loved one."

Sara and I approach two graves, and she hands me a rose. The names on the headstones read *Mary Forever and Edgar Forever*. I take a deep breath and place the rose between them.

"It's my fourteenth birthday today. If both of you were alive, would you get me a gift? Sara has been doing a great job taking care of me."

Sara takes my hand and we walk home to bake my chocolate birthday cake. As promised, Ruth and Walter come over with presents. We sit around the cake with the candles lit, and after they sing to me, Sara tells me to make a wish.

The room is folding over again, like a story starting a new chapter, and I say my wish:

"I wish I can meet a superhero in real life."

Michael Colon

CHAPTER 3

This place, I know I've been here before. In a field of dead flowers, there stands a gigantic estate that looks like it can house one hundred families. The estate is surrounded by a forest of white trees. On my left is a children's playground coated in ice. The swings, slide, and monkey bars have seen better days.

As I walk toward the mansion, I hear the sounds of kids telling me to wake up and come home. At the front doors, a sign reads: *Indigo Orphanage: A home for those without one.*

Before I knock, the doors open, and a blast of cold air hits me.

I enter Indigo Orphanage. The walls, ceiling, floor, and furniture is covered in ice. The sounds of people screaming and crying echo like sirens in a tunnel. I run toward the exit, but it's not there anymore. The halls keep stretching onward with no end in sight.

I yell for help, and the floor turns into a black

liquid that I sink into. The black ooze is freezing cold. The shadow person I keep seeing walks up to me. I reach out, hoping it will help me, but it pushes my hand away and gets close to my face. Its eyes are glowing red.

I wake up in my bedroom. The alarm clock is ringing. I turn toward my action figure tucked in bed next to me. Blood runs from my nose. I have such a headache. I get up, and in the bathroom, I watch the water run from the faucet and down the drain. I focus on the blood to clear my head, but it turns black, just like the ooze from my dream.

I shouldn't even be awake right now. I need to get back to sleep because my first job interview is today. I splash water on my face and throw myself into bed, staring at the superhero posters taped to my ceiling, wondering if I'm good enough to get the job. I juggle questions in my head about whether I can handle the responsibilities of working.

Finally it's time to get ready.

I adjust the tie Sara pre-knotted for me, so all I have to do is tighten it around my collar. Sara was able to afford cheap but oversized dress clothes so I'll look presentable for the interview. I look at myself, dressed up, and still don't feel confident.

The Greatest Comic Book Tale Ever Told

Not feeling confident is how I'd felt all through my freshman and sophomore years. I'm still an outcast from an outcast district that's becoming more like a landfill every day, with trash from the rest of the city piling around our homes. Irontown is doing its best to wipe us off the map. I hear people talk about the monsters that live deep within the landfill. Anyone who goes in too far never comes back, not even the masked gang members.

As I stare at myself in the mirror, I remember what Sara said about puberty. I did get taller, and I have acne on my face, but I'm still weak. Sara told me I need to go through these changes before becoming a grown man, but I don't feel closer to being one. I still can't protect anyone, not even myself. I'm just a loser who isn't great at anything except being a comic nerd who gets taken advantage of.

I walk past the service tents that provide rations to the starving in our torn-up neighborhood. The families standing in line look miserable.

On the cross-district bus, I look out the window while adjusting my tie and repeating what I'll say to the store manager. But no matter how many times I rehearse a proper introduction, I hate the way I sound.

I get off the bus and walk through the Metro District, surrounded by Irontown's cleanest streets and busiest people. Everyone here has a job. There are no service tents. There's purpose in every step.

I approach a group of men in nice suits, smoking cigars. Behind them towers a skyscraper. Ads hang in the lobby windows for the financial investment businesses inside.

"Pardon me, guys. Do you know where I can find Greenberg's retail store?"

They look at me with disgust.

"You look like one of those animals from District Seven in that oversized, horrible suit. Are you? They should all be kept in cages."

A lobby attendant steps out. "Good morning, gentlemen. Can you please smoke a little farther away from the premises? It's building policy."

"We own multiple companies in that building," one replies, "so we'll smoke wherever we want. Get lost, bellboy."

The attendant puts his head down and goes back inside. The group tells me to get lost, too, and I do, without proper directions.

Eventually, I find Greenberg's Wholesale Store mere minutes before my interview. I give three hard

The Greatest Comic Book Tale Ever Told

knocks at the employee entrance and recite what I'm going to say. The locks click, and I take a step back.

A security guard opens the door and looks at me with a sour face. "What do you want?"

"I was called in for an interview with Mr. Greenberg."

"Show me your ID."

"Since I'm only sixteen, I have my school ID."

He sucks his teeth and takes my identification. "I'll be right back."

The big metal door slams in my face. I guess I just wait.

After a few minutes, the security guard returns with a man in a baseball cap and a toothpick dangling from his mouth. He hands me back my ID. "I'm the supervisor here. Follow me."

The supervisor and I walk through the inventory room, which is the size of a warehouse with boxes stacked everywhere. I don't know if I can handle working in a place like this. Based on the enormous size of the inventory room, and all eight floors of retail space, I know for a fact the workload will be too much for me to handle. We reach Greenberg's office. His name is printed in gold on the door.

"You may enter the office. Good luck," the

supervisor says.

He leaves, and I adjust my tie one last time.

I enter the office. Mr. Greenberg is sitting in a black leather chair with his feet up on the desk, showing off his bright green checkered socks that match his suit. Everything in here looks expensive and retro. "Sonny, have a seat."

I sit down, keeping a blank expression on my face, but my fingers are waging war with each other in my lap.

Greenberg extends his hand, and I remember Sara telling me to always give a firm handshake. I reach across the desk and grip his hand tightly so I don't seem like a wimp. He leans back in his big leather chair and puts on his reading glasses to review my lackluster résumé.

"Thank you for coming in today, Sonny Forever."

"It is my pleasure, Mr. Greenberg. I mean, thank you, Mr. Greenberg. I mean—"

"You're the youngest person I've interviewed in a long time, being that you're sixteen."

I know my résumé is far from impressive. The only information on it is the school I attend and a paragraph Sara helped me write, stating that I'm open to work and eager to learn.

Greenberg places the résumé flat on his desk and slides it back toward me. He leans in closer.

My hands are shaking.

"Sonny, I'm trying to find a reason to hire you. You don't have any work experience, and you're still in high school. It gets busy around here, and I could use someone willing to work full-time. You live all the way in District Seven, which is, let's just say, not known for producing the most outstanding candidates. Nothing personal. So...why should I hire you?"

Now's my chance to not sound like a loser. "Mr. Greenberg, I might not have any work experience, but anything you want me to learn, I'll do my best and work hard. I'm in high school, and I know I need to take my education seriously, but if you need me full-time, I'll come here straight after school and do the night shift. During the summers, I'll work full-time. Even though I live in the landfill district, I promise I'll make it to work on time. You can trust me." My throat is dry. It took every ounce of courage to say that.

A big smile spreads across Greenberg's face. "Good answer, Sonny. I have a full-time position for you. You seem like a good kid trying to make a buck. I'll probably need you on weekends, too. That won't be an issue, right?"

"No issue at all."

Greenberg rubs his chin, staring me down. I do my best to maintain eye contact, even though it's awkward. He gets up and guides me to the office door. "Come back Monday to begin your on-the-job training with Supervisor Thomas."

Thomas, the man who escorted me here, meets me outside the office. He still has the toothpick hanging from his mouth.

"Congrats on getting the job. See you Monday after school."

I leave Greenberg's and look up at the skyscrapers. I should feel excited about getting my first job, but I don't. I probably won't last the first day.

The more I look around, the more this city doesn't feel real. It looks like something out of a coloring book. This world doesn't feel like it's the way I've been told it is. Everyone marching around me looks like a comic book character in their own story.

My life feels like it's being told about me.

On the cross-district bus, I adjust my tie and look

up at the sky. I see people floating in place. The bus enters the landfill area and passes through a panel. While going through the panel, I glimpse a world where heroes and villains battle each other between the frames.

My life is nothing but panels I feel forced into, and this hopeless feeling keeps getting more intense.

I sit at the foot of my bed, holding my hero toy. I never outgrew the action figure Sara got me years ago. Other teenagers my age want to hang out and party. I don't like doing those things. I press the button on my hero's chest, and it lights up golden, like rays from the sun.

"Do you ever feel alone?" I ask it. "If I wasn't your friend, would you fly out this window?"

I place my action figure next to the wooden bird model Ralph gave me years ago. Playing with the moon pendant in my hand, I think about how cool it is that Marylee and Franklin are officially boyfriend and girlfriend. They should be here any minute now.

The cross-district bus pulls up. When they get off, they run over to me and hug me. Franklin lost so much weight that he looks fit now. Marylee doesn't have her thick glasses or braces anymore. They both matured so much. Unlike me.

Michael Colon

"Both of you have changed during the summer, yet, I'm still the same."

Marylee says, "You got a little taller."

I don't feel like I've matured the way my friends—or other teenagers at school—have. As I show my only two friends a side of Irontown that's deprived of love, I pull my moon necklace from under my shirt. I'll always keep this precious symbol of our friendship. "Hey, guys. Remember when we first got these moon necklaces?"

Franklin says, "This is like our wedding ring. A vow that'll always last."

Marylee turns to him. "Like a wedding ring? I like the sound of that."

Franklin laughs nervously. "Uh oh. I messed up now."

Marylee hits him on the arm. She still hits hard. Marylee is in the honor society, and Franklin's on the wrestling team.

Marylee asks me, "Do you ever think about trying to get a girlfriend, Sonny?"

"I don't know, Marylee. No girl I've seen would ever want to be with me."

"Nonsense, bro," Franklin says. "You could totally have a girlfriend. You're a great guy."

The Greatest Comic Book Tale Ever Told

At the old railroad yard, we sit on top of one of the carts and read comic books together. The three of us lie side-by-side, holding up our comics, sharing our favorite parts.

Afterward, we make shapes out of the clouds over the polluted river that wraps around half of the landfill district. This river is the most toxic in the country. Plastic and waste float on top of the water. The water itself looks like black sludge. Only death thrives in it.

Marylee runs over and throws a rock into the river.

Franklin picks up a rock next. "Watch a pro do it." He throws it farther than Marylee did.

I throw mine even farther than Franklin's. I don't even see it splash. I've never thrown anything that far before. Maybe it's because I was thinking about that moment passing through a frame, seeing those beings trying to get through. Questioning what this world is really about.

We walk farther into District Seven, toward the giant landfill. Mountains of trash rise as tall as buildings.

Marylee clings to Franklin's arm. "This place feels dangerous."

We hear growling in the distance.

"Guys, maybe we should stop walking."

A louder growl echoes, causing us to take a few steps back. That roar doesn't sound like any animal I've ever heard. I wonder what beasts live in the trash. Some say Irontown put monsters in the landfill to eat District Seven residents who get too curious, thus slowly killing us off.

I tell them, "District Seven will be a giant landfill one day. Many people will die. Me and Sara...if we lose our home, we'll have nowhere to go. We'll become like the people you see on the sidewalks, living with no purpose."

We leave the landfill and go to my room.

Franklin is amazed by all the comic posters taped to the walls and ceiling. "Your bedroom is like the downtown comic shop. So many epic moments from different heroic stories."

We play cards and board games for the rest of our time together. Marylee goes to use the bathroom, and Franklin holds my hero action figure.

I ask him, "Have you ever wondered what your purpose is in the world? Lately, everything doesn't seem the way it's supposed to be."

Franklin sits on the bed next to me in silence.

The Greatest Comic Book Tale Ever Told

"It's okay," I say. "You don't have to answer."

"I'm just processing how to answer. To be honest, I've never thought about life that way. But I think we all have a role to play, and that includes you."

I walk my two friends back to the bus stop. Before they get on the cross-district bus, we tap our moon pendants together.

I return to my room and sit on the bed, staring at the game we left on the floor. Game pieces are scattered across the board.

I pick up a puzzle piece token.

Am I meant to fit into this world?

I lie in bed...and I'm back at Indigo Orphanage. In the middle of a frost-covered hallway, I hear children calling my name. I follow the voices until I reach a door that leads to the basement. As I descend the stairs, the temperature drops. At the bottom, a pair of red eyes wait for me.

I run back up, but the door slams shut. An unknown force pulls me down into the cellar.

Down here, I find a room with a bunch of chairs facing a brick wall covered in comic book pages. The shadow person sits in one of the chairs, legs crossed, staring at the wall. I sit beside it. More kids fill the seats.

Michael Colon

A counselor stands in front of us with a stick. Every time an orphan looks away from the comic-covered wall, the counselor smacks them. The comic illustrations move. I hear smacking noises. Watching the pages animate puts me in a trance. I sink through the floor and into black waters filled with floating garbage. I try to swim up, but ghostly arms drag me deeper...until I wake up in bed.

I run to the toilet and vomit. I need to be ready for my first day at work tomorrow, and this isn't helping. I step out of the bathroom and find myself halfway through another comic panel.

I'm tired of how my life forces me to live page by page. I move the rest of my body into the scene.

I'm in my work uniform, walking to Greenberg's after school. At the back employee entrance, I adjust my collar and give three hard knocks.

The security guard opens the door. He doesn't have the same scowl as last time. "Good afternoon. I'll radio Supervisor Thomas now."

"Thank you, officer."

He calls Thomas and places the radio back on the charging port. "You seem like a really nice kid. Be careful. Some of the people who work here can be real pricks. Look out for yourself first."

The Greatest Comic Book Tale Ever Told

Supervisor Thomas comes out. "Ready to train, Sonny?"

"Yes, sir."

Thomas guides me into the employee locker room, which also serves as our break room. He points out my locker. "After you get situated, meet me at the loading dock."

I place my superhero bookbag in the locker and hear some remarks from coworkers about how goofy I look in my uniform.

At the loading docks, Thomas introduces me to my co-workers. I'm the youngest by decades. Most of them have beards and grizzled expressions.

My job is hard labor: to load and unload trucks, move merchandise to the inventory room, and help sales associates when needed.

For the next three hours, I lift heavy boxes—most of them with help—and run back and forth across the store to stock items on shelves.

By the time Thomas checks on me, my entire body aches.

"You work hard, Sonny. I respect that. Take your thirty-minute dinner break, then back to work."

I head to the break room, feeling a little proud of myself.

I pull out my peanut butter and jelly sandwich and sit alone with my comic book. The other employees glance at me like I don't belong.

Someone turns on the small TV in the corner of the room. A news segment shows the poor conditions of District Seven. The reporter says we're hanging on by the last of our resources, soon to be a graveyard of trash and dead bodies.

The workers curse at the screen.

One of them turns to me. "I hear you're from that shithole district. Just so you know, we have standards around here. We don't have time to deal with animals like you."

I get up and finish my meal on the loading dock.

I look up at the sky, wishing a hero would come down and save my district from this abuse. More neighborhoods are getting torn down and turned into landfills for Irontown's expansion. They want to wipe us out.

I hear fighting behind one of the trucks. I go to check it out and see a hero wrestling a monster. They crash into the truck again and again.

Before I can call Thomas, they vanish.

After my break, I power through more grueling hours of labor and nastiness from coworkers.

The Greatest Comic Book Tale Ever Told

When my shift ends, I grab my belongings. The same workers glare at me like they want me to drop dead.

I walk by Officer Jackson and smile. "Have a good night, Officer Jackson."

"Hey kid, you don't have to call me officer. I'm just some guy making chump change."

"So am I. But my friends say everyone is important. Right?"

He nods. "I like you, kid. See you tomorrow."

I step outside and look at my name tag in my hand, feeling out of place in this cartoon-colored Metro District. Another panel opens at my feet.

I'm tired of walking through these scenes.

I ask a few people nearby if they can see the opening, but they all look at me like I'm crazy.

Then someone shoves me into it.

As I fall, I see a group of people in all-black suits and sunglasses. Who are they? Why do I feel like I've met them before?

I fall through panel after panel, all rough days at work. Coworkers bully me. They vandalize my locker and call me horrible names.

I keep stepping through more panels...until I'm finally back in my bedroom.

Face down on the bed.

Exhausted from lifting boxes, and from carrying people's hate.

I close my eyes...then wake up in an icy hallway.

In this frozen hall, I try to open each door, but they're all locked. At the far end, the shadow being with glowing red eyes waves me over, holding open a door.

I walk inside, and it closes the door behind me.

The shadow shows me a comic book. On the page: a drawing of me as a child.

The shadow flips through the pages, showing me and other foster kids being led into a basement. Men and women in black clothing and sunglasses perform tests on us, looking for a "special child," one who might possess supernatural abilities, like a hero or villain in a comic book.

These people belong to an organization with major influence over what goes on in the world. They operate from the shadows, and they fund Indigo Orphanage.

In one panel, there's a room filled with examiners and counselors. It's labeled high priority. In the center of that room—strapped to a chair—is me.

The shadow throws the comic book at me, and

The Greatest Comic Book Tale Ever Told

I'm suddenly inside that secret basement room.

A dozen examiners, counselors, and guards are monitoring me. The people in black suits are called the Examiners.

The little-boy version of me is strapped to a chair, staring at a screen repeating loops of abstract patterns.

One Examiner says, "This one might be the special child we've been searching for. The alpha and beta waves we're receiving from him are showing two distinct signals of reality."

Another asks, "If this is him...what do we do now?"

"First, we continue suppressing the boy's memories using our secret technology. That'll give us access to his dreams. We'll monitor him, and if things get out of control, we'll handle it. Next, we ensure the right person adopts him. There's a woman named Sara Goodings from District Seven. It's a risky move, but I'll pull the strings to make sure it works. If he wakes up to the truth about who he is and what this world really is, we'll lose our influence."

I can't believe what I'm hearing.

Is this real?

The ominous shadow being wraps its freezing arms around me from behind.

"It's all so real."

I wake up.

Step out of bed.

Fall into another panel.

This time, I'm opening the fridge. There's barely any food inside. I close it, trying to gather my thoughts. Sara left money for groceries, so I head to the local supermarket. It's the only lifeline for the neighborhoods around here.

At the store, I check off everything from the grocery list Sara gave me. While waiting in line, I see people begging outside. No one pays them any mind.

When I leave, a mother and her little boy approach me. They have dirt on their faces and wear torn clothes. "Please...do you have any food?" she asks.

I split the bread I bought and hand them a few pieces.

The woman falls to her knees. "Thank you so much. What is your name?"

"My name is Sonny."

"You are our hero. Thank you for saving us, kind soul."

She takes her son's hand, and they scurry off with the scraps.

The Greatest Comic Book Tale Ever Told

When I get home, I drop off the groceries, and I see the Examiners from my dreams watching me outside.

I step out, and they use a device that looks like a film projector to create a comic panel at my feet.

Now, I'm at Walter and Ruth's.

Is my life real? Are the people in it real?

Ruth waits for me to take a teacup. I get up and run to the front door, hoping to catch the Examiners. But they're gone.

I go back inside and sit beside Ruth.

"Is everything okay?" she asks.

"I don't know."

While sipping tea with Walter and Ruth, they ask me what I want to do after high school.

I have no answer.

I guess that makes me a loser.

Only losers don't know who they want to be, right?

I keep glancing at the basement door. It creaks open and shut from a draft.

Walter says, "I need to fix that door. That noise keeps waking me up at night."

Ruth looks at me. "You seem very curious about what's down there. Why don't you check it out? All we have are stories to pass down. Maybe you'll find something to add to yours."

Walter gives her a look, like he didn't want her to say that.

I get up and stand at the top of the basement steps. Below me: blackness. And a pair of red eyes.

I walk down the creaking stairs. The air grows colder.

Something brushes against my forehead.

I pull the string for the single lightbulb on the ceiling.

Boxes. Dust. Old belongings everywhere.

And...a chair.

Bolted to the floor.

In front of it, taped to the brick wall, are pieces of torn paper. I walk to a stack of boxes and wipe away the dust. Each one has a date written in black marker.

"Look over here," a voice says.

In the corner, the phantom leans against a stack of boxes, whistling. I walk over, and together we open one.

Inside: old clothes I've outgrown. One shirt says Indigo Orphanage. Beneath the clothes is a folded newspaper article from the Irontown Daily.

The Greatest Comic Book Tale Ever Told

Before I can read it, knocks come from upstairs. Walter calls out, "Everything good down there, Sonny?"

I quickly fold the article and slip it into my back pocket, then close the box. "Yes. I'm fine. I'm coming up."

Walter comes down, looking around the basement with disappointment. "No matter how much I organize this place, it's always dirty. Let's get out of here and into the light of day."

After spending time with them, I walk to the abandoned railroad yard. I sit inside an empty train cart and unfold the old news article.

It says Indigo Orphanage somehow froze over...due to an unknown cause.

I flip the paper. Through blot marks and faded ink, I read about children being abused for the sake of a secret project led by a mysterious organization in search of a "special individual." The case went cold, and Irontown moved on.

The intensity of these memories from my time at Indigo gives me a painful headache. My nose begins to bleed. In my mind, a montage of drawings flashes by, a younger version of me being mentally and physically abused by the Examiners.

They bring in a TV broadcasting all the world's evil: murder, betrayal, theft, and every sin committed by humanity, but also the good.

The stimulation from the video warps the room. My younger self briefly transforms into a red-eyed shadow being.

As ice covers the room, one Examiner turns off the TV and puts a blindfold over my eyes.

I snap out of the montage, breathless.

I leave the railroad yard. An opening in reality appears in front of me. The shadow being stands beside me.

"Just what am I?" I ask.

It takes my hand and guides me into the panel.

Now, I'm sitting in church next to Sara.

The angels painted on the walls don't save the starving people from the landfill district.

This all has to be lies.

Priest Williamson steps up to the altar and speaks into the microphone. He talks about good and evil battling around us every day. It's an invisible supernatural world, just as real and important as the physical one.

He calls on the congregation to pray for others.

When I close my eyes, I see the orphanage. Dead

bodies. Frozen solid.

I open my eyes and gasp.

Sara is deep in prayer, rocking back and forth.

When we get home, we sit on our worn-down couch with ripped cushions and watch TV. During a commercial, I look over at Sara, feeling ready to ask her. "What happened to Indigo Orphanage? The one you picked me up from."

Sara turns off the TV with the remote.

"I'm not sure what you mean."

I take the article I found in Walter's basement and hand it to her.

Her smile disappears. She's in shock.

"Sara...what is this?"

"I don't understand what you're getting at."

"You're not telling me something. Please be honest. Why didn't you tell me what was going on there?"

Sara looks distraught. "I wanted to protect you. That's why I didn't say anything about the horrible things they did to you...and those kids."

She walks away and returns with a scrapbook. She opens it and shows me pictures from her childhood. The last few pages are of us, after she brought me to District Seven. The very last photo is of my biological parents holding me as an infant.

It's the only picture ever recovered of them.

On the back: the address to Indigo Orphanage.

Sara says it was deconstructed after everything that happened, officially for "mysterious reasons." She believes that place was cursed by the devil for what went on inside.

I sit on my bed and write the address down, just to remember it.

CHAPTER 4

I open my eyes. I'm at the front doors of Indigo Orphanage. Everyone here is in a good mood, and the children are playing with one another. I walk into the orphanage, and it's busy with counselors and children doing activities. This place is amazing. I'm glad I'm from this home for lost and unwanted children.

Suddenly, a chill goes down my spine.

"It's a lie. They want you to forget."

Indigo freezes over. I see two frozen people holding hands. They are my mom and dad.

I wake up with my face buried in textbooks and comic posters on the new study desk Walter made for me. I have placed the desk near my window so I can always have a view of the sky. On the glass, the remaining pieces of ice are melting. Winter is always so cruel to my district. When the temperature drops dramatically, it cripples so many families, considering not everyone has enough money to pay for heat. I move my textbooks and posters out of the way and lean forward on the little wooden desk to watch the water droplets fall off the melting ice. There were many times we had to wrap ourselves up in anything we could find to keep from getting hypothermia.

At the railroad yard, I stand on top of one of the train carts. Patches of snow lie beneath me. I raise my arms in front of me as the sun rises and think about flying. What an experience that must be. I close my eyes and feel my feet leaving the top of the shutdown train.

Am I finally doing it? Is this seriously happening?

I open my eyes. My feet haven't moved.

I lie back on the cart, holding my comic book up, thinking about how I'd made it to senior year of high school. Thinking about the dreams I have. I wonder where life will take me next.

After an hour of daydreaming, I hop off the train cart and fall through a comic panel...into my work uniform for another long shift at Greenberg's.

My life feels like an endless loop of repeating circumstances. A movie that sometimes I wish could be different, where I don't have to be me.

Since I never stick up for myself, the other workers at my job mess with me and demand help from me in a rude manner. I never did anything mean to them. Seems to be the same story no matter where I go. People take advantage of the weak.

At the end of my shift, we all form a line to clock out. The cleaning workers and sales associates cut in front of me. They usually cut because they know I'll never say anything.

In the break room, while grabbing my things from my locker, a breaking news segment airs on the TV. The news shows St. Michael's Church—the only church in my district—in flames.

The sad thing is there are no people, or firefighters, trying to put out the blaze.

I leave work and step into a scene panel where I walk in the direction of the church. I smell sulfur in the air. In the distance, people are crying near the rubble of what's left of the house of worship. Preacher Williamson is on his knees, holding some of the rubble in his hands. He bows his head and calls out to God for answers, but just like when I pray, there is no answer.

The bad people who hide their faces did this, according to what I'm hearing. The bad people from the landfill stole everything, then burned it to the ground. They probably feel there's no point in having a church here since no angels are looking after us. All we have is ourselves.

I stick around until it's just me and Williamson left.

He keeps his face buried on the ground, sobbing. Preacher Williamson finally struggles to his feet. "My life's work is gone."

"I'm sorry for what happened to your church. If only a hero could come and make things better around here."

"That hero you speak of is God. I still believe God has a plan for good to win."

"How can you still believe in God after what just happened?"

"The devil may have burned my church to the ground, but my faith will never be destroyed. We must always believe that good will win when it's all said and done. Be well, Sonny, and always have faith. Give your mother my blessings."

Preacher Williamson leaves.

Now Sara doesn't have a church to go to.

I walk to a brick wall and punch it, causing the concrete to crack.

How in the world did I do that?

My hand should be broken, but my knuckles don't have a scratch on them. When I hit the brick wall, I thought about how the wall didn't feel right. Like it's a small part of the big lie I have to live every day.

I walk to the old railroad yard. The Examiners are here. I run away, and the shadow being opens a scene panel and grabs my arm. The Examiners run toward me, shouting that they didn't open that scene and that they don't want to go through it.

The shadow instructs me to jump through so I can finally go back home. I quickly jump through, but one of the Examiners grabs my wrist. I pull as hard as I can but can't break free. I manage to get half my body through the panel, so it starts to close. The Examiner lets go, and I fall.

Now, I'm outside of Irontown High.

Franklin honks his horn to call me over.

I feel like I'm reliving memories in an endless loop that I haven't experienced yet. A life that's on repeat. I get up and walk over to the car.

Marylee rolls down the window. "Sonny, are you sure about this?"

"I'm sure. It's not too late to back out of this trip. I'll understand and not take it personally. I'll find another way to get to Indigo Orphanage."

Franklin unlocks the car door for me to get in.

He takes out his moon necklace. "We're in this together. I'll never go back on that promise we made during freshman year to always have each other's backs."

We give each other our signature fist-bump of friendship and drive off...back to where it all started for me.

I gaze out the passenger window as Irontown's skyline gets smaller.

Franklin asks, "What's on your mind, buddy?"

"I'm not sure what to expect when we get there. I don't even know what I'm looking for exactly. I just need to go back to where I came from."

Marylee says, "We might not be able to relate to how you're feeling, but that doesn't mean we won't try our best to support you on this trip."

I'm glad they're my best friends.

The main highway through the lush Indigo area has forest on both sides of this seemingly never-ending road. We drive around for an hour, only to find dead ends. We're running low on gas, so we stop at a small town called Indigo Hills to look around for any indication the orphanage is near.

This small town is well kept, and people enjoy each other's company. The complete opposite of the landfill slums.

Franklin says, "Let's see if any of the town's people here can help us."

We must've stopped a dozen people here in the suburbs, but nobody knows anything about the orphanage. They deny such a place exists. We walk into a pawn shop, and the man at the counter carefully polishes an antique statue of a bird.

"Always good to see new faces in this town. How can I help you all?"

I ask, "Do you know where Indigo Orphanage is?"

The shop owner looks at me like I said something horrible. He almost drops the antique and has trouble placing it on the shelf properly, his hands are shaking so badly. "I've never heard of the place before. I'm sorry. I can't help you."

We all stare at him, wondering why he reacted like that.

"You youngsters should visit the hills. They're scenic this time of year."

I feel like we're being lied to.

"What if I told you I'm one of the kids from the orphanage?"

He takes a few steps back and stares at me like

I'm a monster. The shop turns cold, and Marylee and Franklin hold themselves. The antique shop owner sees his breath in front of him and begins to hyperventilate from stress.

I slam my hands on his table, causing all his antiques to tremble...just like he's trembling.

"We always welcome outsiders, but your behavior is not acceptable."

Marylee and Franklin can't believe how I'm acting, but the anger is making me feel strong. And I like it. I place my hand next to a gold model of a ship and slide it closer to the table's edge.

"Sonny, stop," Marylee tells me.

I stop moving my hand.

Franklin pulls me away from the table and tells the shop owner, "We're leaving."

Outside, Franklin holds onto my arm, and I push myself away.

"You can't do that, Sonny," Marylee says. "We'll never get anywhere threatening folks like that."

"I know you're frustrated for not getting the answers you want," Franklin adds. "But we won't give up because we're all in this together. You're not alone."

"I'm sorry for acting the way I did. Let's keep

looking for a little while longer."

I hear the whispers of children calling my name from one particular direction. The children's voices are telling me to come home to Indigo Orphanage.

We go to the town's scenic hills, and the whispers get louder. At the top of one of the hills overlooking a vast expanse of trees, I hear the kids' voices from one distinct area. The voices tell me to go through the forest.

"Guys, I know the way. If the orphanage isn't where I think it is, we'll go home, and I'll never go looking for it again."

We leave the small, peaceful town and drive farther into the forest until the road becomes a dirt path. As clear as day, I hear a voice call to me, so I tell Franklin to stop the car. He parks off the side of the road. There's a trail that leads farther into the dense forest where I see some white trees. Franklin removes shrubs and branches from an old sign that directs people to Indigo Orphanage along this exact trail.

"Guys, we can't leave the car unattended. Both of you stay here and watch each other's backs."

Marylee says, "You know we can't possibly let you go in there alone."

I take off my moon necklace and hand it to her.

"I'll come back to retrieve my necklace. I promise. I expect you to put it around my neck then."

Marylee takes the necklace and goes back to the car, slams the door shut, and looks away from us.

Franklin tells me, "I'll get her to understand. Just be safe, and if we don't see you in the next hour, we're going to come looking for you. That is our choice."

I give Franklin a fist-bump and walk into the forest.

The deeper I walk through the white trees, the more I think about getting lost and starving to death.

I stop walking to compose myself, and then I hear the kids' voices again. I hear leaves and twigs break around me, so I hurry to hide behind a tree.

I peek around the trunk.

It's the Examiners.

How did they know I was here?

I wait for them to go farther into the woods, and then the voices call from a direction away from where they went. I follow the voices.

I exit the white trees to an open field, where I see a giant mansion. This is the same Indigo Orphanage from my dreams. On the front doors of the home, there's a notice of demolition that will commence the next day.

The Greatest Comic Book Tale Ever Told

Looks like I made it just in time.

I enter Indigo Orphanage.

This place still has leftover ice on the walls and floors. I walk down the hallways lined with old photos of lost kids and the people who used to work here.

A chill makes me hold myself.

Suddenly, the front doors burst open.

The Examiners are here.

"Follow me." The phantom takes my hand and guides me to a room that does not have ice on the door. "They won't find us here. I'll keep us safe."

The Examiners walk right past the room without checking inside.

"I made this room invisible to them for a short time."

When the coast is clear, the shadow guides me to the basement, the same one I saw in my dreams. The phantom with bright red eyes runs ahead of me into the cellar and tells me to hurry. There are room doors halfway open, and in each of them, rusty chairs are bolted to the floor, and old comic pages are taped to the walls.

There is one room the shadow guides me into. There's a chair. Dozens of broken TV screens and worn-out comic book pages cover the brick walls.

I sit in the chair.

The shadow being takes all the pages and organizes them in front of me. "It's finally time for you to wake up to the world you exist in and see who you will become."

The comic pages on the wall form a timeline of my entire life.

From the abusive experiments...

To when Sara picked me up...

Until now, sitting in this chair.

The Examiners have always been around in the shadows, a shadow government altering the events of my life.

My memories have been suppressed, my dreams manipulated so I'd never remember any of this.

The shadow tells me that dreams are a window into the soul. Dreams are a fabric of reality that reveal alternate truths.

The Examiners are part of a shadow organization that wants to influence every part of my life to maintain control over this world, a world created by me, which I don't fully understand.

They don't want me to expose who they are.

They don't want me to fix the repeating loop of this reality...

The Greatest Comic Book Tale Ever Told

Or the comic book universe where actual heroes and villains exist.

Because I'm from the original reality.

A comic book universe.

But nobody knows this.

The shadow says, "All those slaves to the shadow government are walking around asleep, with Irontown being a symbol of ignorance. They want to stop you from waking up, like you have been, thanks to me. I'm not the villain. I'm here to give you the power to be strong in this disillusioned society, a city that also wants to wipe out your community in District Seven. You're going to have no choice but to wake up very soon."

There's a pounding on the other side of the door.

Everything has been a lie.

Sara was set up by predetermined fate to take me in so I'd forget.

There is no God or angels.

There is no purpose, except to look out for yourself.

The shadow being shows me, on the brick wall, the destruction I'm destined to cause when I finally wake up...and fully accept it.

I see all the events that will happen.

Michael Colon

I know what I must become. I rise from the chair and punch the door off its hinges.

The Examiners fall down.

They scramble to their feet and run.

Alarms blare, a call for evacuation.

And then I see myself...

A little boy who finally snapped from the abusive experiments, now transformed into the shadow being. I follow the mini-shadow as it walks, making everything around it freeze solid. I'm no longer walking alongside the monster.

I am the monster

One that can't be stopped.

All the doors at Indigo Orphanage lock.

The lights flicker.

Counselors and orphans try to escape, but their fate is sealed. Wherever I walk, people turn frozen solid.

I find my parents helping evacuate kids.

They're counselors.

I watch them die instantly.

Frozen, holding hands.

I froze the entire orphanage.

I killed many people.

I follow the memory to the front doors.

The Greatest Comic Book Tale Ever Told

My younger self lies unconscious. A group of Examiners hover over me.

"We're going to wipe his memory clean," one says, "and cover up what happened here."

The memory ends.

Everything becomes the present again.

I'm traumatized by the past...and by what I know I'll do in the future.

I stand outside the orphanage.

The Examiners have guns drawn and pointed at me.

I want the worst things to happen to these people.

I'm enraged.

There are flashes of muzzles...but the bullets bounce off me.

I look down.

The shadow is wrapped around me, smiling. My body is protected.

I disarm the Examiners.

Beat them.

All of them.

They flee into a panel.

"Now that you know the truth of your life, you need to take advantage," the shadow phantom says.

"You're supposed to become me. I can only intervene for so long. I need you to wake up...and forget about Sonny."

Then, it vanishes.

I walk back through the woods, processing everything that happened.

I sit down against a tree, visualizing the terror I'm destined to cause.

I see people running...

Screaming...

A storm overhead, sweeping in the horde.

The phantom said an event will happen first, something that leaves me no choice. It didn't say what. Maybe that's on purpose.

I calm myself.

I can't keep Franklin and Marylee waiting.

I exit the forest and return to the road.

Marylee gets out of the car and runs over to hug me.

Franklin says, "We were a few minutes away from looking for you."

Marylee puts the moon necklace around my neck.

We get in the car and drive back to Irontown City.

Franklin asks, "Did you see what you needed to see, brother?"

"Yes. I did."

Marylee says, "Let's never do something like that again, please."

"We won't have to."

The rest of the ride is silent.

I see my world for what it is...a fiction story, full of lies and hurt, with my fate predestined for me.

They drop me off in front of my home. I stare at the doorknob, feeling numb, then walk inside.

Sara is doing a crossword puzzle in the Irontown Daily.

I sit beside her and watch her search for the right word.

"Hey, Sonny. How was your time with Marylee and Franklin?"

"We went to Indigo Orphanage."

Sara stops. She folds the newspaper in her lap and looks at me. "You said you were going to the Irontown Mall with them. You lied to me."

"You're right, Sara. I did lie. But you lied to me first. I found Indigo Orphanage. And I was shown things. The reason you found me wasn't because of God and the angels. You were manipulated by them.

They steered the events in your life to fit their agenda for me. Because they knew what I will become. I'm the reason that place closed down."

Sara takes my hand and leads me outside. We sit on the steps. She looks up at the stars. "I'm sorry that I lied to you, son. Before I found you, I felt like I was just going through the motions of life. Waking up every day to the same loneliness. I never told you that. I needed to be strong for you. But then one evening, a night just like this, I saw you. I was trying to find comfort with God when I found you, accompanied by those mysterious people in black suits and sunglasses. I couldn't make out their faces. They looked like people...but something about them wasn't human. It was like you fell from the sky, right to me. Like it was meant to be. I was supposed to be the one who found you. God must've heard my prayers to adopt a child. It was impossible to get approved by Irontown's orphanages. Our district. My job. My living conditions. But then...there you were. As soon as I held you for the first time, I couldn't let go. Those people disappeared into the shadows. I convinced myself they were angels. They only told me one thing. To never mention Indigo Orphanage. Or that they were the ones who brought you here. You had no name. So I named you Sonny, after my grandfather. He was a good man. A hero to many in this district. It all felt like a bad dream. Until I found you. I'm sorry you experienced what you did at Indigo. I don't know exactly what you saw. But what I do know is we found each other. And that's all that matters."

I nod slowly. "Let's go finish the crossword puzzle together, Sara. I want things to feel normal tonight."

We go inside and fill in the blanks of the Irontown Daily puzzle together.

The last word: Faith.

I step outside again, holding the wooden bird model Ralph gave me years ago. I squeeze it. It breaks in my hands.

A few pages flip. Sara helps me with my prom outfit. She adjusts my bowtie and reminds me that prom night is a once-in-a-lifetime event.

Ever since visiting Indigo Orphanage, I've felt more alone than before. Sara hasn't brought any of it up since I told her.

She combs my hair and smiles. "My baby is so handsome. The girls will be after you."

"I don't think any girls are going to be running to me."

"Just take in the night. Life happens fast, and these moments are fleeting. At least your two best friends will be there. Enjoy this precious time together."

I give her a hug.

She heads to work, expecting me to tell her all about prom.

I close my eyes and open them in front of Irontown High, the panel closing behind me.

The guys have nice tuxedos and expensive flowers.

The girls wear lavish dresses and glittering shoes.

Everyone looks like they belong.

And I'm here. Oversized tux. No flowers. No date.

A banner hangs across the entrance:

"Irontown High School Prom Night Extravaganza."

Maybe I can make up a story for Sara. Maybe I don't have to go in.

My feet start to move backward, and I bump into Marylee. She's standing behind me, hands on her hips, and clears her throat. "Um, excuse me, Sonny. Where were you going?"

Franklin adds, "You look nice, bro. I can't wait

to get this prom night started."

Marylee is stunning in a bright red sparkly dress and lipstick. Franklin wears an all-white tuxedo. They both take my hands.

We walk into Irontown High together.

In the gymnasium, the DJ plays music under spinning disco balls.

Lights dim. The energy is contagious.

Franklin heads to get punch.

Marylee turns to me. "Since freshman year, I've thought about what prom night would be like."

She sees me lost in thought and punches me in the arm.

Hard.

How can I say I live a normal life when I've seen what I've seen?

Nothing is real.

This world is an illustrated fiction tale.

And those shadow government people? They'll never stop watching me.

Marylee's cheeks flush as Franklin returns.

I can see how much they love each other. It's beautiful. It's something I'll never have.

The DJ gets on the microphone. "Alright everyone. Welcome to your Irontown High Prom

Night Extravaganza. Let's make this night a night to remember. Let's celebrate!"

The crowd erupts in cheers.

Marylee says she'll dance with me after the first song. I wait on the side while she and Franklin take the floor.

A girl I've never talked to taps me on the shoulder. "Wanna dance?"

"Thanks for asking, but I'm waiting for my friends."

"Ew. You're gross." She walks away to a group of guys and points me out. The guys surround me. And then...in the dim corners of the gym, I see the Examiners fading in and out. No one else sees them.

The second song is about to start.

Marylee comes storming over with Franklin behind her. She tells the guys to leave or she'll have them kicked out.

They back off.

Marylee grabs my hand and pulls me to the dance floor.

Franklin gives me a thumbs up.

Without Marylee, I wouldn't have stepped on that floor. She teaches me some simple moves.

The lights flash.

The music pounds.

Franklin joins us and we jump around.

I let go. Fully. And just like that, the night ends.

Outside the gym, everyone walks away with their dates. The DJ packs up. Marylee and Franklin wait for me by the exit.

I tell them to go ahead, then I walk around the empty gym, past glitter and plastic cups. My hand brushes the food table. The room turns cold.

"You know it's almost time, right?" the shadow says.

"Yeah. I know. No way to avoid it. It's who I have to become. Even if I break the hearts of the people who love me."

The entity vanishes.

A janitor walks in. "Shouldn't you be at a wild after party? Why are you still here?"

"Just...taking it all in."

When I get home, Sara is asleep on the couch. I sit beside her and adjust her blanket. "Sara, you were right. I'm glad I went to prom. I had a great time with my friends. I'll always remember it. But now I have to become something I don't want to be. Even if I tried to explain to you what I experienced at the orphanage, it wouldn't matter. Maybe if I explain it while you're asleep, it'll make more sense."

She stirs but doesn't awaken.

"We are all born into a pre-written destiny, like characters in a fiction tale. The pages will turn, and life will drag us to wherever we must go...because the story says so. There is no God. There is no Devil. Things just...happen. My destiny is to change Irontown forever. And it's going to break a lot of hearts. I'm waking up...for the first time in my life."

I rise from the couch while Sara sleeps peacefully.

I rip off my bowtie, open the door, and fall through a series of scenes:

Senior graduation, fast-forwarded.

Me walking on stage...receiving my diploma. Walking out of Irontown High with my friends, watching the sunset.

We talk about our futures.

Franklin will study business.

Marylee wants to become a vet.

Before I can answer, I see it.

Irontown.

Destroyed by a storm.

Freezing winds knock everything down.

A horde of monsters sweep in.

Franklin says, "Don't worry, Sonny. Most people

don't know what they want right after school."

Marylee adds, "You'll find your purpose. And you'll be great at it."

I mumble to myself, "And everyone will bear witness."

Michael Colon

CHAPTER 5

I open my eyes and immediately hug myself because of the freezing temperatures. Irontown City is in ruins, with people trying to keep warm around small fires. There are hundreds of lifeless bodies on the street, and all the homes are wrecked like a raging category five hurricane came through. I look at myself in a broken mirror on the ground. My reflection is in pieces of who I am and who I will become. In this decimated Irontown City, the citizens salvaging supplies notice me and become filled with fear, so they run away. I smile as the skyscrapers crumble.

I wake up staring at my high school diploma that Sara hung up. A year has passed since I graduated. Marylee and Franklin started their first semester of college. I'm not sure what is the point of me going to college, knowing what I know now. I walk around with this foresight, waiting for the inevitable to happen. What is the point of pretending like I'm about to have a normal life when I'm meant to become the devil that others pray away? I clench my fists and grind my teeth, thinking about the inevitable. I'm the storm that will impact Irontown City. It's the only way to keep this story going. Irontown wants to wipe away my district by flooding it with garbage, so I'm going to do the same to them.

I keep mumbling to myself, hearing the screams of terror from my dreams. I close my eyes to calm down, and when I open them, I'm walking to work.

I stop at Irontown Comic World, and through the window I see Oswald sweeping the floor, like usual. On the front glass display, new comic stories preview evil villains. The Metro District erases in certain areas and redraws itself around me. I use two fingers to brush the outside of the Comic World store, and the crayon colors get on my fingers. That spot I rubbed off is now black and white. I rub the colors back onto the side of the shop. This is why the shadow government wants to keep me asleep.

I enter Comic World, and Oswald gives his usual greeting to his most valuable customer. "Sonny, if you need anything, let me know. I expanded the place for more variety. Enjoy."

I walk over to the new villain section that advertises the most powerful evil characters in the comic book universe. I've never seen so much evil on display for sale. As I stare at the comic covers of monsters, customers come around me to purchase them. The shadow hugs me and whispers in my ear how we can't wait until we become more than I am now.

Oswald comes over to me with his broom. "I almost had to turn into one of these monsters last week when someone tried to break in and steal my stuff. I happened to be doing inventory late that night, and this metal broomstick came in handy. They saw it and ran."

"How would you feel if you had to be the bad guy and hurt them?"

"I wouldn't like it. But I have to do what I must to protect what I care about."

I walk to the exit.

"Hey, Sonny, are you okay?"

"Not really."

Outside Comic World, I see a lady with holes in her clothes, begging everyone for money, but nobody looks at her. I walk up to the woman and stare at her. She looks at me and asks for money.

"Soon you won't feel this way anymore. This city will be in the same place you are." She doesn't

Michael Colon

understand what I mean and keeps asking for money. "Everything will make sense soon."

At work, I stare at my hero bookbag inside my locker. My coworkers' conversations at the loading dock and the customers asking me for help mean nothing. It will all mean nothing.

After work, I walk past Officer Jackson while he writes a security report. "Everything okay, Sonny?"

"I'll let you know tomorrow."

"If you need someone to talk to, I'm here to listen."

At home, Sara is organizing the place and tidying up. She has a big smile plastered on her face. She must have good news. "My sweet boy. How was work?"

"It was okay." I go to the fridge to get a bottle of water. I plan on locking myself in my room.

"You're not going to ask how my day was? Or what news I may have?"

I stop and turn halfway to face her, waiting for what she has to say.

"Well, Sonny, since you asked, I got a promotion at my job. Now we can have some more spending money to do things together. Things around here won't be as tough for us."

"That's cool." I turn back around and brush off

her news like it's nothing.

Sara comes into my room and sits down next to me. "Sonny, I don't understand what has gotten into you. You've become more detached as the weeks go by. This is not the same boy I remember. It's like you're here, but checked out, with your mind elsewhere. This concerns me as your mother."

I hold Sara's hand and rub my thumb gently on her knuckles. "This world we live in isn't what you think it is. This world has no justice. Some people have to be good and some have to be evil in order to find a place in this story, in our comic book world. The characters in this story aren't aware that they're still asleep. I am finally waking up."

"And what exactly does any of that mean?" She shakes her head and takes a breath. "Sonny. I don't like this kind of talk. Please just stop."

"I will stop."

"You've come such a long way. That high school diploma is something you should be proud of. You have to look deep into your heart and see how special you are for yourself. I can call you special all the time, but you must see it in yourself. I still believe that no matter what you choose to do, college or no college, whatever you do will leave this world in a better place than it was before."

"Sara. It's nice out. You don't have to leave for work yet. Let's go for a walk."

Sara gets up and looks out the window, smiling. "Yes, let's hang out for a few before I have to go."

We walk through the war-torn neighborhood, making shapes out of the clouds on this beautiful spring day. One cloud is the shape of a heart. I've never seen a heart-shaped cloud like that before.

"That is a giant heart. I bet your heart is bigger," Sara says.

"How so?"

"Because the physical size of a heart doesn't determine how strong it is."

We go to one of the local playgrounds that has trash all over it. This playground is not safe for kids, but it's all we have. Sara and I sit on the swings, slowly rocking back and forth.

"When I was a little girl, your grandparents always pushed me on the swing. When Ruth got tired, Walter would push me and never get tired. I never wanted to get off the swings, and neither did you. But the other kids wanted their turns, and it's only fair."

Sara gets up and pushes me lightly. As I rock back and forth on the swing, I replay the events that were revealed to me at the orphanage. I can never truly enjoy any moments in my life until what comes to fruition. None of this will matter by tomorrow.

We go to the polluted river to look at our district's crooked and broken skyline. It's actually not much of a skyline at all. Sara mentions to me how tomorrow is not promised, and to make the most of the moments we experience right now. "I'm so glad we got the chance to have some mother and son time before I have to go. I feel so much love from God and the angels right now."

"I still have a hard time believing in God and the angels if superheroes can't be real."

"Well, maybe they are the same. We won't know until one actually shows up."

"Did you ever think I'm delusional for believing superheroes live in the sky somewhere, watching over us?"

"No. I would never tell you that."

Sara looks at her watch, and it's time to head back so she can get ready for work. As we walk home, she finds a hula hoop in a small pile of trash and explains how she used to be really good at hula hooping when she was a little girl. She rotates the hoop around her waist fast for multiple rotations before it falls. I try to do the same but can only spin one rotation. Some neighborhood kids walk by with dirt on their faces and some wearing masks, laughing at me because of how silly I look hula hooping. Sara tells me to ignore them and not let anyone ruin a nice moment.

She tells me not to worry about what others think and to always be my beautiful self. I walk Sara to the cab, and before she gets in, she gives me a long, firm hug. Sara kisses me on the forehead and leans her forehead on mine. "Remember, son. Always be your true self. Nobody can take that away from you. And no matter what, I will always be here to guide you. I love you more than anything."

"I love you, Sara."

My smile slowly straightens. I know what's to come, so I go into my room and cry. I take my framed high school diploma and smash it. A ripple opens in front of me, and the shadow person steps out of the rip in reality. I rock back and forth, thinking about Sara pushing me on the swing for comfort, while my hands are over my eyes. The longer I stare into the panel, the more intense and heavy these emotions run rampant inside me. I'm petrified of stepping through this scene. This is the scene panel where I start to become strong. But the pressure and gravity of the

The Greatest Comic Book Tale Ever Told

painstaking situation I was told to endure is setting in on me. I just want to go to sleep, wake up, and all this goes away.

I try to run out of my room, but the shadow grabs me and drags me to the panel by my ankle. I scream and plead to approach this another way, but it tosses me into the panel as the shadow government breaks into my bedroom. I land in a black void with my bedroom door in front of me. In this void, I hear the sound of someone screaming, tires screeching, and metal crashing. I step through the other side of the door, and I'm outside my job. The colors of my world melt off, and everything is in a black-and-white monotone.

Police officers come over to me. Supervisor Thomas, Officer Jackson, and my loading dock coworkers all look distraught. The store workers who mess with me look sad too. I step into the cop car, and we speed through traffic. I can hear my heart pounding in my chest.

The cops escort me into the Irontown Hospital emergency lobby. Walter and Ruth hold each other, hysterically crying. I have never seen them both like this before. A few nurses escort us to a patient room with doctors waiting for us.

The phantom puts his hand on my shoulder, and I see Sara's last moments after getting into a car accident in the same cab she took to work from when we hung out. I experience leftover memories of Sara dying, repeatedly. The ominous shadow tells me that he froze these memories to help me be who I have to become. That he purposely never told me all this time how I would have to wake up. This page keeps turning back and forward, allowing the sorrow and anger of watching her suffer hit me. Just like on the swing set, the shadow person makes this moment happen over and over until I feel like I'm losing my mind.

Finally, the page of this moment stops flipping back and forth.

In the patient room, I hold Sara's hand at her bedside, traumatized. Doctors tell us she is in a coma, and these machines are keeping her organs from shutting down. Walter and Ruth are petrified and don't know what to say to the doctor. A few of my teardrops fall on the side of the hospital bed. I'm thinking about everything Sara has ever told me about God and the angels. Where are God and the angels to save and protect her? Why is God letting this happen? Maybe God and the angels are all one big lie, like my life has been from the very start. Superheroes watching over us behind the clouds are a lie too. The good guys don't make a difference in this world.

Walter comes over and puts his hand on my shoulder. "Grandson, this is a traumatic moment for us. No matter what happens, we are still a family and will stick together."

Walter has a look of defeat on his face and probably doesn't believe his own words. The doctor comes into the room and explains to us that there is nothing they can do to make Sara better. Her internal organs are severely damaged. The life support machines will keep her in a coma, and if they wake her up, it can only be for a very short time.

As I hold hands with Walter and Ruth, the nurses turn off the life support machines and send an electric shock to the brain and heart to make her conscious temporarily. Sara's eyes open slowly, and a big smile goes across her face when she sees us. The doctor tells us that he will give us some personal time with her before we have to say our goodbyes.

Walter and Ruth embrace their daughter.

"We could have been better parents for you, my beautiful daughter," Walter says.

"Don't say that, Dad. You're the best father

anyone could have asked for."

Ruth says, "I'm so proud to call you my daughter. You have turned out to be the best mother ever."

"You're the best mother, Mom. I'll watch over you, for eternity, with God and the angels."

Ruth latches onto Walter, and they can't compose themselves as they walk away to cry in the corner of the room. Sara tells me to come to her, so I sit beside her, processing everything that's happening.

"Sweetheart, I'm aware that my time is up. God and the angels are calling me home, and I must heed their call. God has a time for all of us to depart from here, and I'm glad I got to be a mother, more importantly, a mother to my special boy. I believe that you will do great things for the people of Irontown City and eventually the world. The world needs a bright light like you to shine bright."

"I don't want you to go."

She raises her hands to touch my hair. "Life is not fair, sweetheart, and you know this. You have to be strong now and use everything that I taught you to become your own man in life. I promise this won't be the last time you see me."

"How?"

"While I was asleep, I had a long dream that I did

not want to end until you guys woke me up. This dream was the most beautiful experience I have ever been part of. In this dream, people praised you for all the good work you did for them. District Seven was also a place with many gardens, and the people were united. During the dream, you stood atop a tall skyscraper, shrouded in a marvelous golden light, as the whole city called out your name."

"I wish that you and I could live in that dream forever. I would leave this life behind to join you in that dream right now."

"Make that dream a reality. Watch over your grandparents and have a family of your own. I'll always be watching over you." Sara turns her head and looks out the window. The grey skies part, and a ray of sunlight shines on us inside the room. The sky looks like it's opening. I see these people floating in place, watching over us. "Do you see them? The angels are real."

"If those are angels, they would come here and heal you."

"We cannot tell the divine what to do. All we can do is have faith and pray that the reasons they show up are for the better. They're inviting me home, Sonny."

Sara's time is up, and the nurses and doctors come back into the room. Walter, Ruth, and I hold Sara's hands as she takes her last breaths.

"I'll always love you, Mom."

This is the first time that I call Sara "Mom."

"I love you too, my son. Thank you for calling me Mom. Remember. Love always wins."

Sara releases her final breath, and her eyes remain fixed on me. She passes away with a smile on her face. I close Sara's eyes, and the machines flatline. The golden ray of light dims, and dark stormy clouds develop with flashes of lightning. Walter and Ruth are on their knees, crying silently, as the medical personnel remove the equipment from Sara's body.

The shadow being holds me from behind, caressing my shoulders. A loud bang of thunder snaps me out of the trance I had entered, and I leave the room. I go into the hospital bathroom and hold both sides of the sink. My reflection has glowing red eyes. The rage, sorrow, and traumatic moment of losing my Sara cause me to drop into a fetal position on the floor. The pain is too much to handle. The pain is so overwhelming that my body is starting to tear like paper and erase away. There are very small pockets of comic panels opening with the shadow organization trying to get to me.

"It's time to let me in. Let go and wake up already," the ominous shadow tells me.

I embrace the phantom, and it opens its mouth of razor-sharp teeth and swallows me. Now my reflection is a shadow with red eyes and razor-sharp teeth. I walk out of the bathroom and raise my pointer finger in front of me. I use my finger to draw a rip in my story and step into Sara's funeral.

I sit alone at the mortuary, giving everyone the impression that I do not want to be bothered. Marylee and Franklin sit next to me as I stare at the open casket.

Marylee grips my arm. "Sonny, we are so sorry for your loss. We have tried to reach out to you as soon as we got the news, but you never answered our calls."

Franklin says, "I have lost a few family members before. I understand how difficult it can be. No matter what, we will always be here for you to help you get through this because we are family."

"This was meant to happen. I don't need any support from you guys." I get up to approach the open casket. This is how it had to be. God and the angels are not real. It was always a lie. The one thing she was right about is that I am special. And I will show Irontown City.

I turn to the rest of the people at the funeral. Marylee and Franklin are hurt by how I treated them. Walter and Ruth don't seem to recognize who I am based on my attitude.

Later that night, after moving into Sara's parents' basement, I sit on a mattress, looking at the wall with ripped pieces of paper taped to it. I put up comic book pages of all the monsters and evil villains who wreak havoc in their worlds.

I sit back down, facing the cellar wall of villainous stories, and smile with satisfaction.

I'm strong. I have finally awakened.

CHAPTER 6

A month has passed since Sara died. Since then, I haven't kept in touch with my only two friends in this world. It's been a month since I had a long meaningful conversation with Ruth and Walter. Sonny Forever has begun his descent into the murky waters. When I close my eyes, I see Sonny sinking farther into the polluted void. I won't be satisfied until he's completely out of sight.

All my life as Sonny, I have been attacked by outside forces beyond my control. Everything about life had its way with me. Life pushed me around, telling me where to go. I stand and look upward at the cellar stairs. I'm going to cause everyone in Irontown to feel my pain. The shadow being was trying to help all along. He was never trying to hurt me. I'm so glad I let the shadow into my heart and mind. However, I'm still not fully who I'm supposed to be.

When Walter and Ruth are asleep, I go outside to embrace the darkness. To spend time with the one who knows what's best for me now. I leave the cellar and stare at the birdhouse Sonny and Walter built together. I was never meant to have a family in a loving home. The trash accumulation is speeding up dramatically on the streets. Half of District Seven is covered in a sea of waste. Irontown wants to erase me from this story, so I need to show the city what true strength is. A group of people sit around a small fire to keep warm.

"All of you will never have to feel weak again. This won't last long. Irontown City will feel my wrath."

"Who are you?"

"I'm the one who is supposed to be strong."

At the railroad yard, I sit in an abandoned train cart, remembering when Sonny used to come here and pretend to fly because that was his favorite superpower. So ridiculous.

I hear footsteps approaching. They must be back for more. They still haven't learned their lesson. A person from the shadow organization attacks me, but I end up beating him. A few more come running over to me. I raise my hands and grab at the air.

I'm no longer forced into scene panels. Now I open them and step wherever I want. I'm a threat to them. I pull into the fabric of reality and hear the sound of paper ripping. I create my own panel with my bare hands.

I step into my work uniform at my job. From the employee locker room to the loading docks, the sales workers still disrespect me, and the loading dock workers still complain about their wives and kids. I remain noncompliant to it all. They all still see the image of Sonny. That will all change once I figure out how to bend reality to the destruction of this city.

After I clock out of work, Officer Jackson stops me. "Sonny, hold up."

I stop walking and give my attention to him.

"I understand you had a significant loss. You haven't been the same at all. Just know that if you need someone to talk to, I'm here for you."

I don't say anything and step out of Greenberg's. Walking the metropolitan avenues, everyone has the Irontown Daily, and on the front cover is District Seven in flames. All of these people are filthy and weak. I hate all of them.

A man on the phone, talking really fast, bumps into me, spilling his coffee on the street. The man points his finger directly in my face, scolding me. I grab him and throw him to the sidewalk. People stop and stare. That man felt comfortable scolding me because he still sees the image of Sonny. Once I fully change, he will be begging at my feet for mercy.

I walk away, nonchalantly, to where no one can see me in an alleyway. I tear into another panel. Now I'm in front of Walter and Ruth's place.

Walter steps out to put the recyclables away in the bin. "Are you up for taking a walk with me, grandson? It has to be better than being in that dungeon all day."

"Sure."

We walk around the neighborhood as he tells me about how much he and Ruth want the best for me. But I already know what's best for me. All I need to do is open the right scene that finally leads to my destiny. I'll have to deal with this ordinary life for the time being. I'm almost there. I can feel it.

"Have you been leaving late at night? Sometimes I hear footsteps and the door unlocking."

"So what if I am?"

"Well, I'm concerned for your safety. And nothing good happens around here at that time."

"I'm fine. Nothing can hurt me anymore."

There are homeless kids running around the garbage, trying to play games using the filthy environment. I see flashes of Irontown in ruins. And it's cold. Very cold.

Walter steps in front of me. "Grandson, this person I'm walking with is not you. I don't know who I'm talking to."

"I guess I'm not your grandson anymore."

"You know that is not what I mean."

We walk back inside, and Walter is still talking about what he wants for me. But they just don't understand. Ruth gets up and comes over to hold my face, but I back away. I go down to the cellar and slam the door behind me. They're just trying to make me weak again. Sonny was nice. Look where that got him.

I lie down on the mattress, and when I close my eyes, I hear the sound of a bird chirping loudly. I don't remember Ruth ever getting a pet bird. I leave the basement and the chirping stops. I walk over to the bronze birdcage in the main room and stare at the blue model of a bird on its perch. I must be hearing things.

I walk to the cellar to dwell in my own thoughts, but the door to get back down there is gone. It's just drywall now. And I hear the chirping again. I lean into the birdcage and ask the blue jay model if it's alive.

"Are you alive?" a voice echoes in the main room.

Now I'm in the cage, glued to the perch. Walter and Ruth walk out of the bedroom to sit and pray. Ruth bursts into tears because of how worried she is for me. Seeing her cry is making me annoyed. After Walter consoles her, they go back into the bedroom.

I hit the bars of the birdcage to try to break free. A bright golden light manifests, and from the golden light, I hear this rumbling voice.

"Are you sure you're free? Are you sure you're strong?"

"Who are you? Let me out of this cage. I'll show you how strong I am."

"Why do you want to leave this cage? You already sold your soul and put yourself into a bigger and stronger one. You think you're strong, but you're not."

The golden light has a strong, warm wind coming from it. I can see the image of a person appearing from the golden light, and a cape sways from his collar.

No. This can't be. Heroes don't exist.

I wake up in the basement, reach up to grab at reality, and furiously swipe down to rend the fabric. In the opening, I see a storyline being drawn and written about someone getting fired.

I poke my head through the panel and see Sonny sitting in Greenberg's office, getting let go. According to Greenberg and Thomas, Sonny has not been contributing the way he used to, arriving late and lacking the skills needed to continue with the store's direction. I climb up into the panel and sync with the penciled-in timeline's event. He and Thomas keep telling me that this decision is not personal.

I walk into an alleyway and sit with my back against the wall. I don't want to be in any light or around people. I sit here until night falls, and that is when I hear a familiar voice say, "That's when I told him I'm in charge around here." Tommy the bully walks past the alleyway with his arms around two women. I follow behind them, seeing red.

Tommy turns around. "Stop following us, freak."

I stop walking and let them go ahead, then follow them from farther behind. We get on a bus, and I sit across from them with my face covered in a hooded sweatshirt.

That doesn't fool Tommy. "I said stop following us. Here's some money. Go away." He throws quarters at me, but I don't move. His girlfriends look concerned.

We get off the bus together, and before he goes

into the apartment building lobby, he tells his ladies he'll handle me and will be right up. Tommy comes over to me and rolls up his sleeves. "Now I have to teach you a lesson."

He must be surprised that I don't run away.

Tommy swings at me, but I easily move out of the way. I grab him, slam him on the concrete, and proceed to pummel him. His blood spills on the sidewalk. My punches are going between his arms as he tries to protect his face. I pick him up by the collar with one hand and set him back on his feet. Then I punch him in the stomach, causing him to keel over.

"Please stop. You win," Tommy cries.

He has tears in his eyes. The big bad bully gets his karma. He used to torment Sonny. Since Sonny still isn't far enough down into the murky waters, his slight presence is enough to bother me, but his hatred isn't stronger than mine. I watch Tommy hold his stomach as he stagger-steps into the condo lobby.

Sonny couldn't have done that to Tommy. I need to hurry and get rid of his memories and some of his feelings before I start to feel sorry for the beaten bully.

In front of me, a dozen people from the shadow government appear. They have guns pointing at me and order me to raise my hands in the air. I raise my hands and pull down a panel that takes us to an abandoned subway.

They shoot their guns, but the bullets ricochet off my body, which is now made of shadow, turning the bullets to puffs of air. My body is virtually indestructible, and I can rip through scenes and create new panels in ways I never did before. The Examiners try to apprehend me, but I pummel all of them with superhuman speed and strength. Even though I have this power, I still cannot bring myself to kill them.

With both hands, I swipe left, sweeping the members of the shadow government hundreds of pages backwards in the story. I turn one page to the right and stand in front of Walter outside their home. "Whose blood is on your hands, grandson?"

I walk past him to go inside. Ruth stands in the doorway to the basement. "Sonny, you should take a bath and clean up."

Walter says to Ruth, "No. Enough of this. He wants to sneak out and act like an animal. There's no point in him cleaning himself up here or staying under this roof." Walter steps in front of me, face to face. "If you can't change back to the grandson we love and care about, then you're going to have to go."

"I hate both of you." I charge to the front door.

Ruth is whimpering about how things should not be like this. "Grandson, we will always love you and hope you come back. But you can't live here if you can't respect us."

"Goodbye." I step out of their home, now without a family—the way it was always supposed to be. My body morphs into a shadow. I'm no longer a person. I close my eyes, and Sonny is out of sight, drowned in the black abyss. I open my eyes. I'm now a monster with dried blood on my hands.

I walk to the city dump. The District Seven landfill. The place where other monsters exist. I walk into the mountains of trash, and the farther I go, the more monsters I hear around me. They peer at me from around the garbage, but when I give them eye contact, the creatures scurry away.

I reach the edge of Irontown City, which is a white canvas stretching infinitely left and right in both directions. I poke the white void, and it vibrates and makes ripples. A comic book comes out from the void. I open it and read about an ancient battle between a hero made of golden light with a fiery red cape swaying behind him, fighting a shadow phantom being with red eyes.

This battle was so intense that it caused the

The Greatest Comic Book Tale Ever Told

planet to form new mountains and islands to rise from the seas. The fight made the sky turn different colors, and weather patterns changed dramatically. The battle reached its peak when both beings collided in an attempt to finish the other off. In that moment of collision, a new storyline formed. An alternate reality. A world that mimicked theirs but was created from that exact moment of collision.

I turn the page in this glowing comic book, and that person is Sonny.

The golden hero with the red cape and the shadow-being were repelled backward with so much force that their world became extremely damaged. The superheroes in that world are in peril. The beings from that world cannot have direct contact with Sonny's reality, but the shadow found a way.

I continue turning the pages, revealing that Sonny's world is a breakaway from that reality. He was technically never born, so he always felt purposeless in life. The reality he exists in is just an accident. The floating people Sonny would see were the reflections of heroes from the other comic world looking over him—but never interfering—because to him, they are merely afterimages.

The comic book dissipates into light fragments,

and I now understand that this white void is the edge of Sonny's world where a choice must be made. Who will win the battle between me and the hero who always matched my strength?

The shadow organization chases after me from a distance, trying to catch up to me with everything they have. I jump into the white paper void and will myself into a manifested reality.

I open my eyes and realize I'm standing in the frozen ruins of Irontown City.

CHAPTER 7

The sky is filled with dark storm clouds, and my creatures, in the form of shadows with bright red eyes, roam the streets. I look at my reflection in a broken mirror. It is completely covered in shadow, with my eyes glowing red. I smile, and my teeth are fangs made for devouring. My fingernails are like razor blades, perfect for tearing apart my enemies. All the garbage Irontown City tried to push up to District Seven in the past is now here. Mountains of trash replace the once monumental skyscrapers. Waste products cover the sidewalks, with toxic black ooze leaking from all crevices of what used to be the greatest metropolitan in the world. The weather never warms up here, so it's always cold.

The citizens of Irontown are at my mercy. The shadow creatures who follow my commands keep these weaklings in check. My goal is to have the entire world under my influence and to get rid of all the heroes who have been breaking into this reality where I rule. Every last one must be erased. Even the idea of becoming a hero must be killed off. All citizens are now homeless and separated from families by design. I give them just enough food and water at my whim to keep them barely alive, to ensure compliance, since I plan on making them all part of my legion. The citizens of Irontown who don't want to be weak and asleep anymore must sell their souls to me.

As I walk to what is left of Greenberg's, my monsters throw themselves on the floor and bow down to me in passing. I stand over Greenberg, who sits amongst the rubble of his store, talking nonsense to himself. I use my foot to nudge him over as he keeps mumbling random words to himself. Such a weak piece of garbage. I go to strike him, but someone grabs my wrist.

"Are you satisfied with the damage you caused, Sonny?" a hero made of golden light asks me.

I pull my wrist away. "No. I'm not satisfied."

I attack the golden hero, but he flies backward. He swoops in, grabs hold of me, and opens a comic panel. I get thrown to where Sonny's friends are. I don't remember their names, but they look like they're starving and unhealthy. Every Irontown citizen lives their life on the brink of death before my horde comes to give them just enough to keep them alive...or tear them apart if they choose to disobey. Irontown's people aren't allowed to have dreams and aspirations anymore. They must live in a nightmarish city, barely holding onto their sanity, or they can give their hearts to me. Sonny's friends are in a line to receive bread and water from my demons.

The golden hero scowls at me. "Look at what your choice did to your best friends. They're suffering. Do you like what you've done?"

"They aren't my friends. I don't know who they are." I shove the hero of golden light through miles of panels to get him out of my sight. So annoying.

A hole in the sky opens, and superheroes in different costumes fly down and surround me in a circle. These superheroes have been waiting for the right time to fight me. I'm sure there are many more trying to enter my world to take me down. But my hate is too strong for them. One by one, they charge at me. One by one, I repel them all.

These heroes come from all sorts of story arcs and use different powers. Sonny used to see them in the sky, floating in place. The once courageous freedom fighters for justice are now all on the ground, groaning in pain like that Tommy punk I had to teach a lesson to. One of the superheroes tries to get up, battered but willing to fight me again. I grab some rocks and shape different blunt objects. In this world, I'm God. I beat this hero up until he begs for my mercy.

I stand in the middle of the downed heroes and see myself as Sonny trying to swim back up to the surface of the polluted water.

I'm not sure how long I've been sinking downward in inky depths. No matter how far I sink, I still haven't drowned. Thought bubbles of memories sink with me. I frantically paddle upward, but arms from the depths of the black oozy liquid pull me down faster.

Everything turns black again.

I hold my head as memories of Sonny hanging out with his two best friends intensify. I can't stand these memories and experiences that keep showing themselves to me. Sonny needs to die for good. In a fit of rage, I roar so loud the earth trembles beneath my feet as I imagine him being pulled farther down into the blackness.

I walk to where Sonny's grandparents used to live. Maybe destroying what is left of this home will speed up the process of getting rid of any essence of the weak boy within me. I tap on the front door, and it falls over, breaking into pieces. A small group of shadow creatures from my legion come running out. Growling, I order them to get back to work. The silhouette creatures with red eyes run off in fear.

I walk inside. The paint is peeled off the walls. There are holes everywhere, and the furniture is ripped apart. I sit on the shredded purple leather sofa and hold a picture frame of Sonny's grandparents from their wedding day. I throw the picture frame across the main room.

In the small backyard, the wooden birdhouse is rotted. My head hurts so much seeing that birdhouse, because I remember Sonny building it with his grandfather. I shove my fist into it, smashing it to smithereens. Then I approach two graves. They must be Sonny's grandparents. I still can't remember their names. I get on my knees and grab at the soft dirt from both graves.

"Both of you would still be alive if you just had woken up sooner. Instead, you died as cowards who exist in nothingness for all eternity because there is no God. There is no good guy that can stop me."

I get up and go down to the cellar of the home. There is an old mattress with rats scurrying around everywhere. This is where Sonny used to stay after

Sara died. The cardboard boxes labeled "belongings" are ripped open and empty. I hold myself and, when I throw my arms outward, a shockwave is released, blowing the house to bits. Nothing of the home is left.

Outside, the hero of golden light graciously floats down, never breaking eye contact with me as his red cape sways in the air. Some of my monsters approach him. The hero spreads this bright light, causing my monsters to run off again.

"Sonny," the glowing hero says. "You're in deep pain. But you're making things worse. I beg you to wake up. We have been down this path many times before, and I don't want to resort to my last option. I noticed you defeated my fleet of heroes pretty easily. I was hoping that they could take care of this. That doesn't seem to be the case, and I'm not going to risk hurting any more of my allegiance of courageous warriors. It is very rare I have to intervene, but it is unavoidable, it seems."

"Who are you?"

"I go by many names. A watcher from heaven, an angel, God, sky guardian, a celestial being, the hero of heroes. What is important is that the forces of good have failed you, Sonny. But we can make this right. Please, let me help you wake up. You think you're

The Greatest Comic Book Tale Ever Told

awake, but you're not. We are caught in a loop of repeating events. This is not our first encounter.

"A very long time ago, I was in a battle with the greatest threat my universe has ever seen. The fight went on for centuries and would have continued until we reached the climax of the battle. With our last blows clashing, the evil shadow being and I created a tear in time that formed this alternate reality linked to mine. You're fighting for the survival of your reality, and I'm doing the same for mine. I stand for good, and I need to end this pointless loop.

"This world does not have direct contact with the hero and villain arcs of my reality. The only thing we can do is make slight appearances here and there without being erased. You beings see a glimpse into our universe through what you call comic books, which all of you unconsciously created. In every loop, you choose the side of darkness. This causes us to fight again. And during our fights, we reach another climactic moment where everything resets. Our realities cannot progress forward and have been stuck for a while now."

"Then I'll finish you and stop this." I run at the glowing golden hero and, as I swing, he evades my strikes like he has seen them many times before. I can't touch him. I throw punches and kick faster, but he evades at an even faster speed. I finally land a blow, sending him through a few homes. The hero flies out of the rubble and lands far more blows on me. Each hit knocks me into another strike at supersonic speeds.

To counter this attack, I summon a horde of monsters to grab hold of the hero while I compose myself. I stretch my shadow arms ahead to grab his neck. I retract my arms, sending myself hurtling toward him, and with the momentum, I thrust my knee into the hero's gut. He goes down on one knee, and I grab both sides of his head, making his body freeze slowly by sending my pain and hate into him.

He grabs both my arms and swings me around, lets go, and I go skipping across the concrete, creating small craters. The hero quickly flies over and grabs me. He blasts off upward into the atmosphere with me and kicks me down into a panel that causes me to fall in front of a home where Sonny used to live with a woman he saw as his mom.

I step inside, and the home becomes alive with vibrant colors filling every inch of this place, with sunlight shining through the windows. Sonny, as a little boy, runs over to the woman as she is making pancakes for him and holds her leg.

"Sara, is that you?" I reach toward the tiny glimmer of light in this black ooze, seeing her reach back to me with a bright smile. "I miss you so much. I want to see you again. Sara, please help me. I don't want to hurt any more people. I want to make things right, but I'm stuck in these murky waters, watching the destruction unfold. I made the wrong choice. If God and the angels are still real, please tell them that, if I ever get another chance to rewrite my story, I'll make it right."

I watch young Sonny and his mother dance around the kitchen while she sings a song from her upbringing. I can feel the love they have for each other. Sonny runs past me and into his bedroom. I follow behind and open the door. Young Sonny is sitting on his bed, reading his comic book. He is so immersed in the story that he doesn't lift up his eyes at all. I sit next to him on the bed, and the room becomes cold, causing him to shiver.

"They aren't coming to help," I say.

He looks at me and runs out of the bedroom, yelling that there is a shadow monster in the room. The vibrant colors fade away from this home, and it's back to being dark and dreary. On the floor is a toy hero that resembles the golden glowing being who thinks he is good's last hope.

I press the button on the middle of the action figure's chest, but it no longer works. I have a memory of Sonny playing with this toy and bringing it everywhere he went. The toy with a red cape used to flash a golden light and would say certain phrases. A few teardrops fall on the action figure. I touch my face and try to understand how and why I'm crying. I'm not supposed to cry and have these feelings anymore. I cause the action figure to become ice and crush it into a fine powder. The entire home develops a layer of ice. I get up and leave the frozen home as it shatters behind me.

At the old railroad yard, I see my demon minions surrounding a person. This must be the usual case of Irontown citizens thinking they can make a stand and actually make some sort of difference. I tell my horde to clear the way, and when they do, I'm still and silent. This person is beat up from what my monsters did to him. In my mind, I hear a conversation between Sonny and a man who was kind to him, a man without a home who gave Sonny a wooden bird.

I ask the man, "Will you give me your heart? Or continue to be pushed around? Will you wake up? Or remain asleep in my nightmare?"

"I still have to believe that there is good in this hell," he says. "I made a promise to a boy named Sonny to wait for the good to come. I never saw myself as being a monster. I can't do it." He coughs up a lot of blood.

I find some joy in that. "Seems to me you don't have a choice. You don't want to die this way. Just take my hand and give me permission to have your soul. If you do, everything will be better."

The man looks at me with hopeless eyes and reaches for my hand. He crawls over to me and continues to cough to the point he is holding himself as blood leaks through the creases of his fingers. Right before he grabs my hand, the golden hero comes and smacks it away. The hero and I commence to fight again, and he flies, holding me, straight through what is left of the Irontown Metro District.

We crash in the middle of the city with people running and screaming for their lives. The golden being releases waves of fire that melt my demons into black ink. The hero grabs me, and we go flying into the decaying skyscrapers of Irontown, causing them to fall over. To protect my slaves from the fight, more heroes come from these openings in the sky to bring them to safety.

I strike and cause the golden hero to crash through mountains of garbage, and he does the same to me. Every time we clash, reality bends and gets distorted for a moment. The fight continues to escalate with each blow, causing more of the city to be destroyed. The hero flies around in a circle so fast that all I see is a ring of light, and the heat gets higher. The ground is set ablaze, and I feel myself burning.

Before catching fire, I cause my shadow body to grow tall and stomp on him. I'm a giant, crushing him under my foot.

I've finally won.

I suddenly feel my foot being pushed upward, and the glowing hero completely pushes me off him, throwing me off balance. I take a long, hard fall, shrinking back. The shadow that was attached to my body left me bare and exposed. I quickly run to merge with the ominous shadow entity again, but the hero puts his foot on my chest, pinning me down from moving.

"Unfortunately, I have to resort to what every superhero doesn't want to do. He leaves me no choice. All my other attempts lead to our battle loop repeating. A near-death experience is the only way."

The Greatest Comic Book Tale Ever Told

The golden glowing hero raises his fist, and fire burns bright around it. Objects float upward because the concentration of energy is affecting gravity. The hero strikes down on my chest, causing my heart to stammer.

My vision fades in and out while the sound of my heartbeat slows down. The hero props me up against a mountain of garbage. My breathing lessens and I slide off to the side, but before I hit the ground, a woman who took care of Sonny catches me.

Michael Colon

CHAPTER 8

My eyes open in the murky waters, and the water is clearing. It is no longer polluted and freezing cold. A warm pressure, glowing gold and red, pushes me up to the surface. I finally breach the waves and feel like I've awakened from a bad dream. Sara, who looks like a glowing angel, holds me in her arms. She wipes the dried blood off my face.

"Mom, I'm scared. I don't want to die."

"I'm so happy you called me Mom. I told you that we would meet again. I've been watching over you with the angels and God. What you've been doing is not good, and it's not true strength. I'm saddened to see the choices you made."

"Can things just go back to how they were? Before I found out everything I did? Before heroes and villains?"

"Not quite, my son."

"So...I'm going to die, right?"

"You're not going to die yet, my son. The Hero

of All Heroes told me that you have another chance to make the right decision."

"Alright, Mom. I'll make the right choice. But how can I be forgiven for what I've done? All the people I hurt. Look at what I did to our world. It's a nightmare."

"The Hero of All Heroes is so strong and mighty that forgiveness can be given if the circumstances are right. You're being given a second chance, and although I would love for you to come to where I am, to have more fun times as mother and son, I know you have to be my special boy in this life first. Because I still believe you are a superhero in your own story. And I can't wait to see how it ends. I have the best seat in the house to watch."

"Alright, Mom. If the Hero of Heroes is giving me the opportunity to reverse all the damage I did, I promise to do what I must to make everything right again. I'm going to miss you."

"I'll miss this moment between us too. But I'm still watching over you, my sweet boy." She brushes her hands through my hair. "Remember, son, love always wins."

"Can you sing me a lullaby like you used to? I'm feeling tired."

The Greatest Comic Book Tale Ever Told

My mother, Sara, sings me one of the lullabies she would always sing when I was scared. It comforts me easily. She rocks me back and forth in her arms, glowing like a beautiful angel, until my eyes close.

Michael Colon

CHAPTER 9

I open my eyes, and the brilliant glowing golden hero in the sky is trying to keep this reality from ripping apart and destroying both of us. The angelic hero has multiple outstretched arms made of its glowing golden energy, holding different places in the air to keep the apocalyptic Irontown from pulling itself apart in all directions. The shadow demon is crawling away from me, breathing heavily.

"Sonny," the golden hero calls. "You did it. Your memories of love and light kept you alive from the near-death experience I had to give you. You need to defeat the evil shadow once and for all. I won't be able to hold reality intact very long. You need to be brave, and you need to fight back."

The phantom shadow stands up, wobbling and looking weakened. "You're making the wrong choice, Sonny. You need me. You're weak without me. Remember all the pain and suffering you went through. Remember how those heroes never showed up when you needed them most. Remember how they took Sara away from you. It's not too late to accept me back. But you have to hurry."

"Her name isn't Sara. It's Mom. And I've always been a superhero. I just didn't know it until now."

An army of shadow creatures of all shapes and sizes surrounds us, and the phantom orders them to attack, but they don't. They don't because they know their leader is no longer in control. I am.

At my command, thousands of monsters are ready to devour the phantom. The shadow being keeps shouting at the demons to attack me, but their eyes are fixed on the phantom.

"Boy. You need to accept me back. Do it now," the begging phantom shouts.

I walk up to the shadow being. "Seems to me that you're the one who needs me. Not the other way around. I know what choice to make."

"Sonny. Make the right choice," the golden hero shouts from the sky, still holding reality together, but losing his grip.

I slowly raise my hand, and the ominous being cowers. Instead of taking the phantom's hand, I point upwards toward the hero in the sky, signaling that I choose a new way.

"Attack," he orders his demons.

The Greatest Comic Book Tale Ever Told

"Too late." I drop my hand and walk away.

The legion of demons all charge the ominous shadow while a dark, murky void, glowing red, opens up beneath them. As they devour the shadow phantom, they all fall into the abyss.

A comic panel opens in front of me, and on the other side lies Indigo Cemetery.

"Sonny..." the golden hero cheers, "this is the last chance to make things right again with the world. I'm sorry you weren't born like most people. Your real mother and father were part of your world's shadow government and wanted to keep you from ever remembering how special you are. The shadow government was a direct reflection of the split in realities that favored the powerful evil you just defeated. You were destined to make sense in your world. You were born to help me fight evil. Go now, Sonny, through your last comic panel and see your real world. Do it for yourself."

I step through the comic scene and stand at Indigo Cemetery. I walk to the two graves to embrace the truth of who I am. The headstones erase before my eyes, as the lie they were. There is a pencil in my hand and a comic book that I previously used, one that caused pain and destruction. One more blank page is there, added by the Hero of All Heroes.

I'm going to sacrifice myself so this destruction can never happen again to Irontown City.

Before I add that to the final page, the hero of golden light and a red cape puts his hand on my shoulder. "No, Sonny. This will not be how the story ends for you. I see your heart and intentions. You were just getting ready to sacrifice it all for the betterment of everyone, and for that, you get a blank page to rewrite the ending of your story. The Hero of all Heroes commands it. The one your mother called God."

I draw and write on the last page, making the right choice this time, and then I hold it out in front of me. The comic book falls out of my hands and lands where the graves used to be.

I wake up in the basement at my grandparents' place. I sit up on the mattress and stare up at the stairs leading to a glimmer of light in the main room.

I open the door to the creaking stairs and see Walter and Ruth watching TV on the purple leather sofa. When they see me, they're so happy that I'm here with them. My lip quivers, and I start to shake.

Walter gets up to comfort me. "Grandson, what's wrong? It's still hard on all of us, I get it. But we are a family and must stick together."

"I'm so sorry for all the pain and sadness I caused both of you, and I'm glad you're still alive."

Ruth says, "You haven't caused us any pain, Sonny. You must have had a bad dream down there in that basement. You should probably get more fresh air, grandson. Come sit with us."

I sit down and put my arms around them. They don't remember anything that happened. Was it all real, or was it all a dream?

"You know what, Grandma, you're right. I had some doozy of a dream."

"You know what your mother used to say. Dreams are a window into our soul and the world outside our own. Dreams are a blessing from God."

My grandfather and I go to the backyard to see the family of birds flying into their birdhouse. It's good as new again.

"Our stories are all we have to pass on," Walter tells me.

"Grandpa, I want to be a hero for everyone someday. I know I can."

"You already are, grandson."

I go to Irontown Comic World in the Metro District and see my two best friends waiting for me in front of the store. I run over to them and jump into their arms. "Franklin. Marylee. I missed you guys so much. I'm sorry I have been out of reach. I was in a dark place. But everything is going to be better. I just know it."

Franklin says, "It's okay. We understand. Losing your mom is a heavy weight to carry. We still love you. If you need more time to grieve, it's okay."

Marylee says, "Let's enjoy each other's company today. The evil in this world can wait until tomorrow."

We enter Comic World, and Oswald still greets me as his favorite customer. My best friends and I browse through comic books just like we did that freshman year of high school. Now we are young adults, ready to take on the world as a family.

I take out my moon necklace as we hold hands, walking to visit Irontown High. It is past school hours, so nobody is allowed inside, although it would be cool just to walk around for a few minutes. I try to convince Franklin to come with me since there's a way inside. The janitor's supplies prop the door open. Marylee does a good job at getting Franklin to stay with her.

I walk the halls of Irontown High School. My sneakers squeak on the freshly polished floors. I slip and bump into a set of lockers, knocking over a wet-floor sign. A folded paper slips out from the bottom crevice of the lockers. I unfold the paper, and it's the comic book page I gave to Franklin our freshman year to hide. On the back of the comic book page is a message written with words glowing gold:

"Sonny, I'm so proud of you, as are all the heroes of my universe. I got the chance to write this message before my world erased away, keeping yours alive. There's a lot that may seem like a blur. You're finally awake and can fight the good fight like all heroes should. Because that's who you are. Even though you broke the loop, your mother could not be brought back. There are certain things that can't be reversed, as they are beyond a superhero's capabilities. The stories of my universe will forever be remembered in the comic book tales you're destined to write."

I fold the page and hurry out of the school to show Marylee and Franklin.

"Sonny," Marylee says, "we were about to go in to get you. I don't want you to get in trouble."

I unfold the comic page and hand it to Franklin. "Remember when I asked you to hide this during freshman year? I told you that if I ever found it, that would mean superheroes are real."

Michael Colon

Franklin says, "Yes, I do remember. I guess that makes you a superhero."

"Look at this." I show them the glowing golden message written to me, but the words are gone. "Never mind."

"What did you want to show us?" Marylee asks.

I decide there are somethings best kept to myself. "It's nothing."

We go inside the only parked school bus on campus grounds to sit together and share stories of what we experienced at Irontown High School. We take out our moon necklaces and tap them together, with the same amount of love from the moon and back, just like what's engraved on the pendants. Franklin takes out a Sharpie, and we write our initials on the interior walls.

Marylee says, "I would like to think our initials will last forever here."

I know the bus driver will wipe them off tomorrow morning. "Only what's in our hearts lasts forever. Like our friendship."

Franklin says, "Wow, this sunset is beautiful. It makes me wonder what life has in store for us next."

I walk all the way back to District Seven and stop by the old railroad yard. I stand on top of a train cart and look at the sunset. I close my eyes and think about flying. I feel my feet leave the train cart.

"Sonny, is that you?" Ralph asks.

I jump down from the train cart and see he has new wooden models. "Long time no see, Ralph. Where have you been?"

"The shelter had some space for me nearby, but after a few years, they shut down, and I had to come back here. What have you been up to? You've grown so much now. Did you meet that superhero?"

"Yes. But it all seems like a dream now. They're real, but in different ways."

"Perhaps you're the hero this story needs. The power is in that big, good heart of yours."

"I'm glad to see you again, Ralph. I do hope the shelter reopens soon. Will you be back tomorrow?"

"Yes. I'll have a new wooden model bird for you. Hopefully you can bring me some food. That pizza looked good last time until those bullies ruined it."

"I'll see you tomorrow, Ralph."

As evening sets in, I go to where I used to live. The house has a "For Sale" sign on it. The garbage has accumulated so much in District Seven that it's hard to walk on the street. I go to sit on the porch and look up at the stars as a warm breeze smothers me like the love my mother used to give me.

I see a star shining brighter than all the other stars, and I reach up. "Mom, if that's you, I hope that you will be proud of me. I will be a hero for the world to see."

I stand on the porch, close my eyes, and stretch out my arms. I feel my feet leave the ground. I'm levitating above the sidewalk. "This is amazing," I whisper.

I want to fly everywhere and show everyone that I'm the first person to fly like the superheroes in my comic books. Everything that I have been through, all that I had to endure, right now I feel alive and ready to make my world a better place. This feeling is so intense that it's making me float up higher.

I take off to the skies. I can see all of District Seven from up here as I soar with my arms stretched out in front of me. The faster I go, the more I realize the reason why I'm flying throughout the neon-glowing Metro District beneath me. It's because, for the first time, I believe in myself and proud to be the superhero of my own story.

I don't feel sad or like a victim anymore. I don't feel like a loser anymore. I'm beautiful in every way because I'm part of life. I'm special, just like my mom said. My bright light will make me be the best that I can be.

I stop thinking these thoughts when I hear a piece of trash fall off a mountain of garbage near me.

I open my eyes.

I'm still in the same place, but I have achieved the true meaning of my purpose in life. And I'm ready to fight the good fight, for Irontown and District Seven.

Because that is what superheroes do.

Michael Colon

Epilogue

I close the comic book and greet my special guest who has just arrived, my beautiful daughter, Sara. "How was your first day of kindergarten?"

She jumps into my lap. "It was so much fun, Daddy."

"Now, let's get ready for your birthday party."

"Daddy? Why is my name Sara?"

"You're named after the wonderful woman who helped me achieve this life, one I'll pass on to you someday. Your grandma was a superhero."

"What was she like? I only saw pictures."

"Grandma was the strongest person I've ever known. Even in the hardest times, when District Seven was a dump, she always put me first, no matter what. That name has been passed down to you, not for you to be just like her, but as a legacy of her strength." I pull Sara into a hug and give her a kiss on the forehead, just like my mom used to give me.

"Daddy? Where are you taking me before my birthday party starts?"

Michael Colon

"Somewhere very special."

"Do they have ice cream there? You know my favorite is chocolate with sprinkles, Daddy. Please, please, please. Will there be ice cream?"

I laugh and hold her hand as we leave my office. After waving goodbye to the downstairs receptionist, I drive to District Seven. My daughter, who turns five today, can't stop talking about the ice cream.

I know my wife is decorating the house for our princess's special day. Franklin and Marylee will attend with their kids, who are Sara's best friends.

We get out of the car in what used to be the slum district of Irontown. It's now the Garden District, with healthy and productive opportunities for all. Nobody feels abandoned. District Seven is growing, with new churches, schools, businesses, and clean surroundings. People are happier.

Every person we walk past waves at us. They see me as the superhero they never had before, the hero that, for the longest time, I never saw in myself. Using comic book stories to motivate the people, I led the efforts to restore Irontown to its former glory, clean up District Seven, and restore law and order to our neighborhoods.

"You sure do have a lot of friends, Daddy."

"When you do good work, you can make lots of friends."

"They all buy your comic books."

"It's not just comic book sales that allow us to have a good life. It's what comic book tales can do for the hearts and minds of those who believe in heroes and angels."

My daughter shrugs. "Okay, Daddy. I'll keep my eyes open for ice cream."

We reach the spot where I have a surprise for her.

"Okay, cover your eyes and I'll guide your steps." I take her to the pristine banks of the once-polluted river. An airplane engine is buzzing overhead, right on time. I remove my hands.

She sees her name written in the sky, the letters forming a cloud-like effect, with a colorful "Happy Birthday, Sara" message.

"Wow! It's beautiful, Daddy!"

I take pictures of her with the sky-writing behind her. These photos will go in my album of memories to cherish forever.

We walk to the tree that stands on a grassy hill, where I also made my mother's tribute. "Thank you for showing me how to fly, Mom."

A tinkling tune fills the air.

Michael Colon

"Daddy! Do you hear it? The ice cream truck is at the playground!"

We rush to the modern and clean playground where I buy us two chocolate cones. After eating the ice cream, I sit down on the park bench and hold my moon necklace while she runs off to play. She's already so brave, such a bright light in the way she interacts with other kids her age. I'm so proud of her.

A page from the Irontown Daily blows my way and catches on my leg. The newspaper is from today's edition, and there's an article about the comic book tale I'd held onto for so long. This special issue I released is about a boy who has to make a very important choice while a shadow government tries to hide the truths of his world from him, a boy who tips the balance in an ancient battle between a powerful golden hero and an evil shadow villain.

I think it will remind the citizens of District Seven how far we have come, together.

I decided to have my comic book company name this special one-time issue *The Greatest Comic Book Tale Ever Told*. I fold the newspaper article, stuff it in my shirt pocket, and notice a cloud that's shaped like a heart. "You're right, Mom. Love always wins."

About the Author

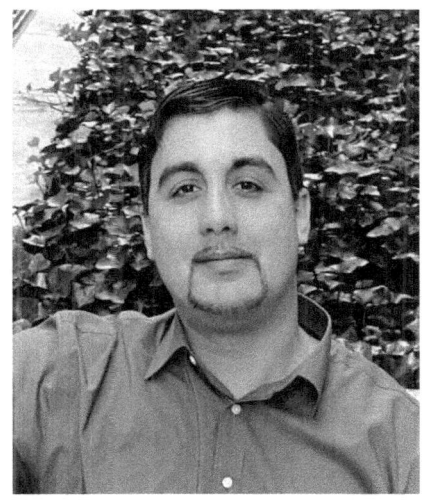

Michael Colon is a creative freelance writer and novelist, born and raised in the Big Apple, New York City. He uses his craft to profoundly impact the lives of others with thought-provoking words that breathe life into his characters. He often equates his writing to painting masterpieces with prose. His inspiration comes from various societal abnormalities, cultural differences, and his own life experiences. When he isn't writing, he enjoys working out, watching sports, visiting museums, and exploring nature trails.

Michael Colon

The Greatest Comic Book Tale Ever Told
More from Michael Colon

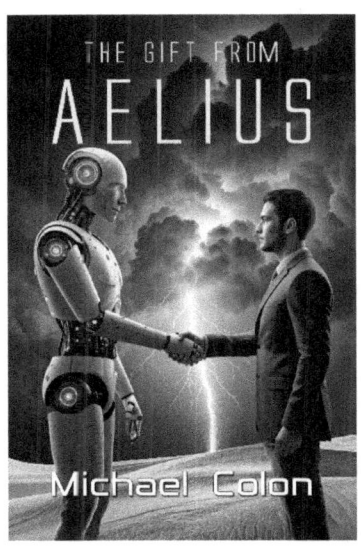

In the not-too distant future, A191, a Codex with artificial intelligence, feels like a misfit in Paradise, a walled city in the middle of an endless desert where humans imprisoned his race long ago. He's not like the others of his kind; he longs to meet humans and make peace with them so man and Codexes can be reunited in the world. These thoughts and feelings are not allowed in Paradise; he risks banishment to the desert by the Overseer A. I. who rules by fear and force. Complicating matters, A191 has a glitch in his programming that conjures up a human boy named Aelius who tells him to go to Old Haven where he will find freedom. However, he's drafted into a rebellion against the Overseer, and as Paradise enforcers close in with orders to terminate him, he escapes the city to wander the desert in search of humans. The journey reveals the truth about his existence, the Overseer's lies, and the consequences of mankind's untethered technology.

Michael Colon

Enjoy more short stories and novels by many talented authors at

www.twbpress.com

Science Fiction, Supernatural, Horror, Thrillers, Romance, and more